Sword of Empire
Praetorian

RICHARD FOREMAN

© Richard Foreman 2013

Richard Foreman has asserted his rights under the Copyright, Design and Patents Act, 1988, to be identified as the author of this work.

First published 2013 by Endeavour Press Ltd.

This edition published in 2018 by Sharpe Books.

ISBN: 9781797549866

CONTENTS

Praetorian

1.

Rome. 171AD.

"He's dead," the stabbed figure overheard as he lay upon the sofa in the triclinium. Blood soaked the scrawny youth's tunic. His usually pale face was now ashen. Junius Arrian had been attacked in his own home. A dozen or so drunks had made their way up from the Subura carrying torches and grudges. The mob had discovered that Arrian was the son of a German tribal chief. And Rome was at war with the German tribes.

Over the past year Arrian had been anxious about being outed as a German, even though he considered himself a Roman having lived and been educated in the city from the age of eleven. He had been sent to the capital, along with his older sister, on the suggestion of the governor of a neighbouring province. It was not uncommon for Rome to educate the sons of its potential enemies – in order to win future allies.

The eighteen year old could not find the strength to open his eyes. His thoughts wandered, as if in a dream.

The attack was a blur. The men had broken in with a couple of axes. Half sought out the owner whilst the rest sought out his valuables and the wine cellar. The bookish youth had frozen in terror upon encountering the intruders, fearful both for himself and his sister, Aurelia. Two wild-eyed men approached him, spitting out curses and cackling. One called him a barbarian and the other judged him to be a spy. Arrian could not remember which one had slid the short blade beneath his ribs. He lay on the floor, bleeding, vainly stretching out his hand, as they took a screaming and tear-soaked Aurelia with them out into the night.

Two slaves, Clarus and Tiro, did their best to attend to their master. Arrian had drifted in and out of consciousness over the next couple of hours. He thought he heard and saw a couple of members of the Praetorian Guard, but again the scene felt like a dream and he couldn't be sure. Clarus had lit a fire and covered his young master with a blanket but Arrian grew increasingly cold.

He understood why he had been targeted. Rome was at war with the Marcomanni and various other northern tribes. The Germans had crossed the Danube and drew first blood in a series of devastating and brutal raids. Twenty thousand Romans had perished, and twice that number had been sold into slavery. Rome had finally mustered sufficient forces to go on the offensive, over a year later, but the war had not gone well for them so far. The Emperor Marcus Aurelius had suffered a series of defeats. Farmhands, firstborns, foreigners and even gladiators, much to the anger of the audiences in the arena, had all been conscripted. Famine had struck and the Tiber had burst its banks in the past few years creating discord. Christians were a growing political and religious force, who looked to serve their God rather than the Emperor. The plague and high taxes were also laying siege to Rome. Marcus Aurelius' co-emperor, Lucius Verus, had recently died. Germans and Christians were, as the Jews might describe them, scapegoats. Romans could and did blame their ills upon the enemy within – and equally they were willing to sacrifice them.

Arrian flicked through the pages of his mind, looking to select a quote from his philosophical studies to help console him at his end. *It is possible to provide security against other ills, but as far as death is concerned, we men live in a city without walls.* Epicurus. *The day which we fear as our last is but the birthday of eternity.* Seneca. He also wanted his last thoughts and prayers to be for Aurelia. She was one of the most virtuous people he knew – at least she had been before finding religion.

The youth winced and arched his back in pain as he re-lived the knife penetrating into his side. He thought that there was nothing he could have done to save himself, or Aurelia. Like the Emperor he had spent his time in the company of philosophy – rather than fencing – tutors. You don't have to fight on the frontline to be a casualty of war, Arrian sadly concluded.

Sweat glazed his countenance. His breathing grew shallow. His dazed thoughts grew even dimmer. Would the afterlife be akin to the forests and grasslands of Germany, or the porticoes and marble of Rome? Arrian wished for the latter. He had made the diverse and wondrous (but far from perfect) city his home. He had embraced his Roman name and lifestyle. Literature, laws, philosophy, civilised conversation – all these would make the afterlife worth living. Ironically his death, at the hands of Romans, could help cause the downfall of the civilisation he so admired. On hearing the news of his passing his father might side with the Marcomanni and their King Balomar – and take up arms against Rome.

The German youth drifted in and out of consciousness again. When he woke he heard Clarus mournfully remark to Tiro, "Get some coins for the ferryman."

Arrian deliriously wondered, had he died and was now hearing these words as a ghost?

2.

A thick layer of sawdust soaked up the wine, spit and various other bodily fluids which stained the floor of the tavern, *The Ambrosial Fountain*. Although it was the dead of night the establishment was still home to a dozen or so patrons. The smell of alcohol, sweat and cheap perfume filled the air. Oil lamps hanging from the ceiling flickered. In the half-light one could still make out the large mural on the wall, depicting certain carnal acts that might have made even Caligula blush.

A couple of haggard-looking whores on a bench turned their heads towards the two praetorian guards who had just entered. Their eyes were bloodshot with drink and the drabs appeared too tired to raise a smile for the soldiers, let alone anything else.

The larger of the two men, a centurion, stepped forward into the centre of the chamber, the studs of his boots sounding across the stone floor. For the first time that night everyone stopped drinking – and took in the soldier. Gaius Oppius Maximus. He wore a red tunic, grieves and breastplate. A gladius hung from his belt. A broad brow hung over dark brown eyes. His short black hair was flecked with grey, his face dusted with stubble. A number of patrons eyed him with suspicion. Maximus returned their stares with a look of thinly veiled contempt, the way a gardener might look upon weeds which needed cutting down.

The centurion's optio, Rufus Flavius Atticus, moved into the centre of the room too. His blue eyes were bright with wit and intelligence and in contrast to his colleague the young man appeared amused, rather than angry. A wry half-smile lined his handsome features as the optio scanned the various faces gazing back at him. Although born to an aristocratic family Atticus had spent many an evening in similar drinking holes to this during his late teens. The former philosophy student had often closed his books early to seek out wine truth. The tavern, as much as the Forum, was the face of Rome, Atticus judged. The Senate would be wise not to ignore all the grievances spouted out during drinking sessions in such places, although they would be equally wise not to listen to all the bile and ill-informed opinions spewed out from the Subura too.

The Ambrosial Fountain was the third tavern the soldiers had visited that evening, passing by scrawny dogs and scrawnier beggars whilst walking the narrow streets. The servant, Clarus, had given Maximus a description of the ring leader of the gang who had abducted the girl. Maximus' orders had come via a letter from the Emperor himself, to retrieve the brother and sister and escort them to his base at Aquileia. The centurion put his confusion and disappointment to the side when he reached the house. It was not worth ruing the fact that if only they had got to the house earlier then they could have prevented the tragedy. "We are where we are," Maximus had stoically remarked. He sent for a doctor to attend to the brother and interviewed the servant about the intruders, figuring that they would take the sister back to a tavern.

Maximus spied his quarry. From his leathery, weather-beaten features and the tattoo of Neptune on his neck Sinius (as the servant Clarus named him) had been a sailor, the centurion surmised. His body was still knotted with muscle. His red hair was doubtless as fiery as his temperament.

Sinius met the soldier's challenging gaze and smiled, or rather sneered – revealing a set of teeth more crooked than a tax collector. His nose was out of shape too, having been broken more times than a poet's heart.

"Give me the girl and that will be an end to it," Maximus said, his voice as hard, flat and direct as a Roman road.

A short silence ensued. Sinius continued to sneer at the centurion. Three of his fellow gang members were still around the table. The rest of mob who had attacked the house had slithered off into the night. The men were part of a carpentry gild. They worked together, drank together and fought together.

"The Praetorian Guard. We used to call you toy soldiers when we served in the navy. Ceremonial puppets, who spent more time polishing their swords than using them. You think you can make or break an Emperor, put a Claudius on the throne and take a Nero off it? In this tavern we're the ones who make or break people. Now fuck off, before I shove your sword up your arse. Although being a praetorian, you might like that sort of thing," Sinius announced. The trio around the table chuckled in support.

The rest of the patrons in the tavern slowly but surely slunk into the corners, cradling their cups. They would be content for blood to be spilled during a fight, but they did not want any brawlers knocking over their wine. One man carried his bowl of stew over to the opposite corner where Sinius was sitting. He happily left his chunk of bread on the table though; he had half-joked to the landlord earlier that the loaf was so hard that it could hammer a nail into the wall.

Maximus pursed his lips and rolled his eyes at his antagonist, seemingly bored rather than annoyed by his response.

"He has a lovely way with words," Atticus drily remarked to his friend, his half-smile widening into a grin.

Sinius grew even more irate. He had inspired boredom and amusement in the arrogant soldiers, rather than fear.

"I have a lovely way with women too. But I won't be shoving my sword up that German bitch's arse later. It'll be something else. Eh lads?" The group once again gave out a drunken, or sycophantic, laugh. Sinius here stood up, revealing the extent of his brawny frame. Maximus sized up

6

the rest of the group sitting around the table. An equally well built brute sat next to Sinius on the side of the table closest to him. His bulk – and the copious amount of alcohol he had drunk – would slow him in a fight but he still would prove a fearsome opponent. He looked like a man who had taken part in many a wrestling bout, although how many times he had been victorious was a different matter. A lank-haired, rat-faced looking man sat opposite from Sinius and fingered the handle of a long-bladed knife. Small dark eyes and a sadistic smirk suggested that the cretin would just as rather put a knife in a man's back as his front, Maximus thought. The final member of the gang, sitting in the far corner, was by far the youngest in the group. He looked about as brave and threatening as a Gallic cavalry officer – and would retreat as quickly as one too. The centurion fancied that he could probably pay the whores on the bench to best the teenager.

"Give me the girl and that will be an end to it," the soldier remarked again, his voice even deader than before.

"I heard you the first time. I'm not deaf, although if seems you may be dumb. What do you want with her anyway? We're at war with the godless barbarians. A good German is a dead German. Her brother is most likely a spy. You should be thanking us, buying me a drink. Can't you see? We got rid of a snake in our midst."

As Sinius spoke he walked forward and fronted up to the officer, looking to intimidate him. Maximus could smell the wine and garum on his breath.

"The only unwelcome creature I can see in our midst at the moment is an ass," the centurion replied matter-of-factly.

Sinius' face folded itself up in rage. He went to draw his dagger from his belt but before the blade was freed from its scabbard Maximus whipped his forearm around and slammed his elbow into his opponent's nose. The landlord winced as he heard bone and cartilage break. *The Ambrosial Fountain* gushed with blood.

Atticus quickly drew his knife, as he saw the rat-faced gang member grab his blade from the table and rise to attack Maximus. With a well-practised flick of his wrist the soldier's dagger zipped through the air and buried itself into the man's thigh. Surprise and pain shaped the man's features – turning to shock as he looked up to witness the optio's fist swinging into his jaw.

Sinius fell to the floor, half concussed. He jolted back to life however when the centurion brought his boot down upon his left ankle, shattering the bone in two places. Sinius snapped his head back and screamed in pain. At the same time the brutal looking drunk who had been sitting next to the gang leader bellowed in anger. Maximus saw a cudgel swinging towards him. Whether it was a reflex action, or deliberate, the centurion raised his forearm. His greave duly deflected the blow of the short wooden club. In reply Maximus butted the pugilist – and then kneed him in the groin (twice) – leaving the brute doubled over and writhing on the floor like a child having a tantrum.

The remaining member of the gang, in the far corner, retreated rather than attacked. His eyes were wide with fear rather than fury. The youth had nowhere to run or hide.

"Where's the girl?" Maximus asked.

"In the back room there," the frightened youth nodded and pointed (repeatedly) in the direction of the door. If he could have told the praetorian in any other way, to appease him more, he doubtless would have.

3.

"Rather than give those coins to the ferryman, I suggest you put them aside for his medical treatment."

Clarus watched, his eyes and mouth wide open, as the smartly dressed doctor entered the room, accompanied by an attendant. His tone had been haughty, aristocratic. His features were slim and sharp, although the doctor would have argued that his intellect and wit were even sharper. Clarus thought that the physician looked more Greek than Roman. His beard was as grey as it was black but the doctor moved with the energy and purpose of a man half his age.

Galen of Pergamum, the Emperor's personal physician, ushered the slave out of the way with a wave of his hand and set about examining his new patient. Friends called the polymath confident; his detractors condemned him as being arrogant. Rather than being something in between, he was both. The Emperor had called Galen "the first and only physician in the Empire." It was a judgement that the doctor and philosopher did not feel the need to dispute.

"Our master is lost. Only the gods can save him now," the slave sorrowfully replied, reverently looking skywards as if he had already started to supplicate Jupiter and Alcipius.

"Well by all means offer up your prayers to save your master, but forgive me if I utilise more scientific methods to cure him. I warrant however that your prayers may well prove more effective than some of the medical practices that my error-filled contemporaries have been known to employ."

The doctor emitted a snort of derision as he thought of some of his contemporaries, who had at one point also been his critics and persecutors. Such had been the whispering campaign – and open abuse – against the freethinking physician that he had been driven out of Rome. Yet he had bravely returned to the capital and gained the patronage of Marcus Aurelius himself. Scientists and lay people alike flocked to attend his public lectures. As well as being engaged by the spectacle of the renowned doctor cutting up all manner of animals (pigs, goats, dogs, elephants), the audience also enjoyed Galen's commentary during which he dissected the practices and philosophies of his rivals. His barbs could cut as deeply as his scalpels.

"He has lost too much blood!" Clarus bemoaned, half burying his master already.

"I dare say that you could set up a practice with such a lack of medical knowledge. All is not lost. The injury need not be fatal. I've treated gladiators who would consider such a wound a mere scratch. Your master may not possess the hardiest frame and constitution, but I can detect a strong enough pulse. As Cicero used to say, where there's life there's hope."

"And do you think that there is any hope that my master's sister will return?" Clarus asked, nervously chewing his nails whilst watching the calm and methodical doctor attend to his patient.

"Yes, both your master and mistress are in safe hands. There are scarce a dozen men in the Empire who the Emperor trusts more than Gaius Maximus. If it is in his power to bring the girl back, he will. Indeed you might rather feel sorry for the men who abducted her. For a score of physicians might need to be called out to attend to the injured, should the gang give Maximus any trouble."

As Galen commenced to clean the patient's wound he thought about the centurion who the Emperor spoke so highly of. Rumour had it that Maximus was a descendant of Lucius Oppius, the famed *Sword of Rome* who had served both Julius and Augustus Caesar. Oppius had a child with a lover, a political agent named Livia. Galen did not know any more about his descendants. He was, however, aware of what had happened to Maximus' immediate family. His wife and children had been victims of the plague. They perished within the space of two months. As well as pitying the centurion for his tragic loss – the Emperor mentioned how much Maximus had genuinely loved his wife – the doctor also admired the soldier. Unlike many of the officers serving in the Praetorian Guard Maximus did not behave like a martinet. Nor did he serve in the army with an eye for political or financial gain. Galen recalled a story that Rufus Atticus once told him: a corrupt treasury official once tried to bribe Maximus – the centurion's response was to break all of the bureaucrat's fingers and arrange for the official to be removed from his post.

The doctor broke off his thoughts concerning the praetorian when he noticed his patient regain consciousness.

"Am I still alive? Or am I a ghost?" Arrian semi-deliriously asked, staring up at the serene and sagacious physician as if he were a god in the afterlife.

"I suspect you are still alive, but if you are a ghost I would be grateful if I could write you up as a case study. Dissection of an incorporeal being may prove somewhat tricky though," Galen drily replied.

Arrian managed a feeble smile. As he came round further the youth realised who was attending to him, having spent many an hour at his public lectures. Arrian had far more questions than answers, but his first was perhaps the most pertinent.

"Will I live?"

"I believe so. Just let me work – and then rest and recuperate. Time heals most wounds."

As he spoke these words Galen once more thought of Maximus and wondered if time would ever cure the widower of his grief.

4.

"If you've harmed the girl in the slightest then I'll cut off your thumbs. If you've done worse to her I will cut off your bollocks – and then kill you," Maximus vowed, as he stood over the still prostrate Sinius. Those who overheard the centurion were left in little doubt that he would make good on his threat. Sinius moved his jaw up and down to respond, but he could only emit rasping groans of pain.

"He's got an even lovelier way with words now," Atticus sardonically remarked, standing next to his friend.

"I'll fetch the girl, if you keep an eye on things here."

The optio nodded and then turned to face the still resolutely fretful owner of the tavern.

"Landlord, make it a large one. I think I've earned it. These ceremonial puppets can put on quite a show, no? On second thoughts, let me buy a round of drinks for everyone, except of course for our friends here who already look somewhat worse for wear," an amused looking Atticus announced, handing over a sum of money that made the evening a memorable one for the tavern owner, for the right reason.

Light sliced into the dank storeroom as Maximus opened the creaking door.

They may take this body but they will not besmirch my soul, Aurelia forcefully told herself.

The young woman in her early twenties was bound by rope to a pole in the centre of the room. Strands of black hair clung to her tear-stained cheeks but there was a look of defiance in her luminous green eyes. Her dress was expensive, made of Chinese silk. The evening's events had sullied the pattern of the garment, but it hadn't been ripped open. Thankfully Maximus had reached the girl in time, before Sinius could have his way with her.

Aurelia took in the figure of the stolidly built praetorian. Had the vile gang sold her to some soldiers? Legionaries often ogled her and made suggestive comments when she went to the market. They were all Godless brutes, the spirited woman thought to herself, whether they were German or Roman.

"Aurelia? Please don't be alarmed. I'm here to take you back to your brother's house," Maximus gently remarked, his tone dramatically different to that of how he had addressed the gang leader.

"Who are you?" the young woman replied haughtily.

"My name is Gaius, Gaius Maximus."

For a second or so the soldier thought he saw that the woman appeared to recognise the name and she stared at him differently, intently. Time stood still. But the fires of distrust and disdain soon re-forged themselves into her expression.

Not wishing to startle the woman by drawing his sword and cutting her loose Maximus untied her. As he stood close to Aurelia, Maximus breathed in her perfume, which scented the air over the odours of the mouldy cheese and stale wine polluting the storeroom. The girl was wearing the same perfume that his wife Julia had used. The fragrance brought back the memory of the campaign against the Parthians, when Maximus would sit in his tent and read over her scented letters. He had closed his eyes and breathed in the perfume, imagining she was there with him. Even now he would sometimes unlock the chest he kept Julia's correspondence in and read her letters. He never wanted her fragrance, or his memories, to fade. A wave of both fondness and sorrow buffeted him whilst Maximus continued to free the woman.

"Have you seen my brother? Is he alive?" Aurelia asked desperately.

"You'll see him soon," Maximus answered in earnest. If Galen had been unable to save the brother then at least he had not, technically, deceived the girl. She would indeed see him soon, alive or dead.

Aurelia did not want to waste any time in getting back to Arrian. She quickly dusted down and straightened her dress. She tucked her long black hair behind her ears, revealing a pale but attractive heart-shaped face, and walked out of the storeroom. The soldier initially admired her fortitude in the face of the trauma she had just experienced, but then considered that the woman may just be in delayed shock.

Her abductors received a withering look of scorn as she passed by them in the tavern. As Aurelia gazed at the youth, however, who had been party to the attack on her home, her expression was one of shame and disappointment – as if he were a lost sheep.

"Drink up," Maximus said to his optio.

Atticus nodded – or tutted – and swiftly drained his cup of wine, wincing after doing so. He didn't know which year the wine was – he just knew that it wasn't a good one. Atticus smiled at the woman as she marched by him but he too received a less than friendly look. He wondered whether she was unimpressed by his drinking, or whether she was chastising him for potentially delaying her. Perhaps it was both. Not even his own mother looked at him with such moral disapproval, Atticus wryly thought to himself – and she knew about his affairs with married women, his gambling, cynicism, wasted academic potential and general profligacy.

Slate grey clouds tessellated together and rain peppered the air as Maximus and Atticus walked ahead of Aurelia and they made their way out of the Subura. The optio glanced back to check on the woman. She still wore a proud, pinched expression on her face. Atticus was unsure whether she was turning her nose up at the stench which pervaded the streets of the Subura, or if she was disdainful of the company she was in. Perhaps it was both.

"Let's hope that the brother's alive when she gets back. The girl's frosty now. She'll be positively glacial if Galen is unable to save him," Atticus whispered to his centurion under the shush of the wind.

"She'll still need to accompany us to the Danube to meet the Emperor, whether he's alive or dead." Maximus had grieved for his wife whilst still fulfilling his duties to his Emperor. The girl could mourn for her brother in transit too if needed, he concluded.

"She seems like a woman more used to giving orders than taking them."

"Perhaps I should have kept the length of rope from the storeroom that they used to tie her up with."

Atticus tilted his head back and let out a burst of laughter, not knowing, however, if his friend was entirely joking or not.

Aurelia barely heard the laughter of the soldier in front of her, absorbed as she was in her own thoughts. Rain fell down her cheeks, masking the tears. Her expression was pinched, due to the revulsion she felt at reliving her ordeal. Images stung her inner eye and turned her stomach. She recalled the scene – and scream – when they stabbed her brother. She could still smell the sour wine on their breath and the rancid odour of garum on the hand that had been clasped over her mouth as they took her back to the tavern. A pock-marked Spaniard had pawed her, saying how much he enjoyed stroking silk. The gang's vile leader had called her a "spoil of war," one which they would all have the opportunity to enjoy. She hated them. All of them. If the authorities did not punish them in this life then they would be damned in the next.

Tears had streamed from her eyes in despair in the murky storeroom. She had prayed to God to save her. Yet rather than the Holy Spirit, Aurelia had been rescued by a ghost from her past – a demon rather than angel, she believed.

5.

The centurion felt somewhat like a captain, whose ship had been becalmed upon the sea. Two weeks had gone by and still they were in Rome, as opposed to journeying north and fulfilling his orders. As keen as Maximus was to deliver the brother and sister to the Emperor he duly deferred to the advice of the physician and allowed time for Arrian to recover his strength.

Maximus assigned Atticus – and a handful of legionaries – to guard the house whilst the adolescent recuperated. He did so partly out of precaution in case the house was attacked again and partly he wanted the guards there to prevent the brother and sister from escaping.

The officer visited the property every few days to check upon Arrian's progress. After speaking to the youth Maximus realised why his Emperor wanted him to escort the Germans to the Danube. They were the son and daughter of the chieftain of the Arivisto tribe. The Arivisto were still to ally themselves with Rome, or the Marcomanni, in the war. Marcus Aurelius would ask Arrian to appeal to his father to side with the Empire – and hopefully tip the balance of power in Rome's favour within the region.

"I would be willing to speak to my father, but I'm not sure how much weight my opinion will carry. I'm not sure I've grown up to be the type of son he wished for. He wanted a warrior, but he's ended up with a philosophy student," Arrian said, with both a flicker of humour and sadness on his pallid face.

"Well, as we will need you to deploy words, rather than arms, you will be well suited to the task at hand," Maximus replied, in an attempt to boost the youth's spirits. He had grown to more than tolerate the boy. Although he wasn't entirely physically developed, the youth was thoughtful and good natured.

Whereas Arrian grew to be at ease in the centurion's company Aurelia would often absent herself from the room whenever the soldier looked in on the brother and sister. Or she would silently gaze upon him with a look of intrigue, or resentment, in her expression. But the praetorian was inured to such behaviour.

"If looks could kill then I would have died a thousand deaths before now," Maximus said to his optio whilst discussing the brother and frosty sister. "It's her father that we need to compel her to speak to, not me."

"You should consider yourself fortunate. The girl responds to me with something far more galling than scorn. She treats me with indifference," Atticus had wryly replied.

*

In order to give Atticus an evening off from guarding the Germans – so he could attend a party hosted by his father, a prominent senator – Maximus came to the house at dusk to relieve him. He encountered Galen upon entering, who had just finished attending to his patient.

"What the prognosis?" the centurion asked. The words had been like a refrain to Galen over the past couple of weeks.

"You will be pleased to hear that he will be fit to travel in a day or so. He should not be over extended in the journey, however. The boy did not possess the most robust of constitutions even before his injury."

"Thank you, Doctor. Now are you sure that we cannot pay you a fee for your time?"

"I'm sure. My motivation is medicine, not money. If ever you call upon me again though try to make the case a more a challenging one, in a less odorous neighbourhood," Galen tartly replied, his beak of a nose still smelling the sewage in the air from a nearby drain.

"I'll bear that in mind. Are you attending the party this evening too? Atticus tells me his father has invited you."

"Spend an evening with senators, talking about politics? I would rather spend an evening attending to lepers. No. The politicians there will ignore me for not being sufficiently important enough for them to speak to – and their wives will carp on about their imaginary health problems. I would doubtless end up wishing certain diseases on the irksome creatures, after discussing the ones that they think they have. Suffice it to say I have declined the invitation. I'm content enough to spend the evening with a good book. I also have to start preparations for our journey together. The elephant that I was due to dissect in a public lecture in a week's time is far more ecstatic about my leaving Rome than I am, but there you are. As many challenging cases as I might find in a warzone, I'm far from enamoured about joining you on your campaign.

"However, it will be a pleasure, rather than a duty, to see the Emperor again. I share your fondness and admiration for him, Maximus. Julius Caesar was great, in regards to his achievements rather than morals perhaps. We may deem Augustus great too. Vespasian was a great pragmatist and Antinous was wise in that by doing very little he did much. But Marcus Aurelius is rarer than them all. For, more than great, he is a good man. But I now worry that I am starting to sound more garrulous than a politician. Or worse still, a politician's wife. Or worse still, his mistress. I will leave you to your duties," the doctor remarked, with a cursorily polite smile and nod of his head, his mind already focused on some scientific or philosophical problem as opposed to his exchange with the soldier.

Shortly afterwards Maximus found himself at the entrance to the house again, bidding a farewell to Atticus. The blood-red horizon was darkening by the minute. Tendrils of smoke began to spiral up into the air from a phalanx of nearby chimneys. The smell was – Galen was right – odorous.

"Enjoy the party."

"I may well enjoy the wines and food tonight but I cannot vouch that I'll enjoy the company. My father's friends talk endlessly well of themselves – and endlessly ill of everyone else."

"It won't be all that bad, I'm sure. You said that wives had been invited too. You might get lucky."

"Lucky would have been avoiding the invite in the first place. But my mother insisted. She used her own version of an officer's vine stick to coerce me – guilt. But enjoy your evening too my friend. Try not to stand too close to the sister. You might freeze to death."

The two men shook hands and Atticus took his leave.

The wine, the news that they would be leaving soon, and Atticus' joke brought a rare smile to the centurion's usually flint-like expression. The smile soon fell from his face when he turned to find Aurelia standing before him, carrying a book. Her dress was plain, her dislike of Maximus plainer. Atticus had said that – should she allow herself to be – the sister could be fiercely attractive. Instead she was just fierce looking, especially in the presence of the officer.

"I want you to know that I am willing to travel back home, not because your Emperor has asked me to, but because my brother has," the woman coldly stated, peering down her nose at the praetorian.

"I've stood in front of thousands of bloodthirsty Persians on a battlefield, all wishing to kill me. How much do you think I'm a-feared or bothered about you standing before me now, wishing to have a tantrum or futile war of words?"

Aurelia stood slightly aghast that the soldier had spoken to her in such a manner in her own house. But before she could muster a reply he had already walked by her, heading towards the wine cellar. She called him a brute in her mind, and remembered Julia again. How could she have loved him as much as she said she did? He was coarse, violent, a non-believer. Aurelia missed her friend dearly, especially given

19

their parting – but thought little about how "the brute" would be grieving for her too.

6.

Music played in the background. Tired and gaunt looking slaves held up lanterns in the garden, providing light and heat for the party guests. Silk dresses shimmered in the moonlight, as the women inside them shivered a little. The low murmur of conversation was occasionally punctuated by the sound of unaffected – and affected – laughter. Around fifty people populated Pollio Atticus' lawn. Merchants lobbied politicians. Salacious gossip and discrete favours were traded. Everyone had an opinion in regards to the war against the Marcomanni, with those who were ignorant of the situation expounding on things all the more.

Rufus Atticus, speaking to his sister Claudia, overheard snatches of a discussion between two elderly, waspish senators.

"...Pius brought Aurelius up to wrestle with philosophical problems, rather than battle barbarians...Taxes are up, the number of desertions is up – and the conscription rates have risen too. The only thing that's down is morale... Aurelius may be a hardworking legislator, but what we need now is a Caesar who is willing to pay the blood price in defeating our enemies... Soldiers are there to be sacrificed for the greater good, that's what we pay them for..."

Atticus (having shaved, washed his hair and changed into a toga) rolled his eyes and wondered how Maximus would have reacted to hearing such criticisms of Marcus Aurelius. He would have made them eat their words he suspected – and may well have knocked their teeth out beforehand. Atticus soon turned his attention to his sister again. Claudia was cynical, sarcastic and pleasure-loving; but it was because of these traits, rather than in spite of them, that he enjoyed her company so much. Other women at the party may have possessed better figures and finer features, but few possessed a greater intellect or caustic sense of humour, Atticus thought. Claudia shared her brother's same intelligent, amused expression. She was the only person in the family who he genuinely admired, or who even half understood him.

"So it seems you will be off to the frontline again soon. I'll miss your company. As you can see, the jewels my girlfriends own sparkle far more than their conversation," Claudia issued, pursing her lips in disappointed resignation as she re-pinned her hair up in a slightly different position.

"I fully intend to come back from the war, although there is of course the ongoing danger of my dying of boredom at this party before the night is out," Atticus countered, whilst nodding in thanks to a slave who filled up his cup.

"You will not be the only one venturing to the front soon, if Cornelius Sulla has anything to do with it. Our local pederast made a speech today, calling for further troops and resources to be put at the Emperor's disposal. He said that he was willing to help oversee the conscription of the young recruits personally, which raised several eyebrows and a number of sniggers in the crowd. But the senator was as bellicose as a Spartan, although given the length of his speech he was not quite as laconic as one. You should have seen it. A vein throbbed in his head and he pounded his fist on his pigeon chest at least half a dozen times to convince his audience of his convictions. He said that he was not one for speechifying, but he felt that the hand of history was upon him."

"If the hand of history was there, I hope that it would have had the good sense to give Cornelius a slap. I'm sure that his patriotic fervour had nothing to do with him being a shareholder in a tin mine which supplies the military."

Atticus could not decide whether he should smile or scowl at the thought of the odious, self-serving senator. Claudia saved him from any decision however as she changed the topic of conversation.

"But tell me more of your campaigns so to speak on the home front. I hear that the social lioness, Lucilla Domitia, invited you to dinner the other evening. Did the lioness get to devour her prey?"

"I declined the invitation. Some vintages are best left on the shelf."

"And what about young Portia? She's far from vintage, indeed she's probably just ripe enough to be plucked off the vine," Claudia remarked with a suggestive glint in her eye, remembering the virginal girl's doe-eyed expression when she spoke about her brother.

"Annoyingly she seemed far more interested in trying to engage me on an intellectual level. She's still in a phase where she wants to talk about poetry or, worse, love. So I'm seeing her mother. She's now a much more happily married woman I dare say, due to the affair. But how is married life treating *you*?" Atticus again gave a nod of thanks to the attentive slave who re-filled his cup.

"Fronto is barely at home nowadays. And when he is there he no longer feels any desire to sleep with me. His life is centred on his business interests. He spends money, rather than time, on me. He doesn't even care that I'm having an affair. In short, married life is bliss at the moment," Claudia replied, eyeing up her father's new bodyguard over Atticus' shoulder – Chen. His broad chest and biceps filled out his tunic nicely. The Chinaman seemed to always wear a sour, disgruntled expression but Claudia believed that she could put a smile upon savage looking features. She had never had a Chinese before and was mildly intrigued as to how he might perform. He had largely been speechless in her presence so far, but perhaps he would open up to her more, in regards to her father's plans, during pillow talk.

"But tell me, how is the widower's life treating Maximus? You must allow me to invite you both to dinner before you head off to save the Empire. You will of course be welcome to depart early, to leave him alone with me."

"You would still end up sleeping alone for the evening. Maximus is still devoted to Julia, for good or ill." Atticus replied.

"The ghost of his wife cannot keep his bed warm at night though."

Claudia grinned and tried to sound glib, but she had more than once thought about being with Maximus, burying her head in his chest and having his muscular arms cradle her. She always felt safe with him – and he brought out the best in her. She liked herself when she was with him. Atticus had introduced the centurion to her some years back. Maximus was a good man, refreshingly untainted by ambition and pretension. She had envied Julia for her marriage to the soldier – and desired Maximus even more for still being devoted to his wife. Too many men were solely devoted to themselves.

Before Atticus could reply he spotted his father making his way towards him from the other side of the garden. He quickly downed his cup of wine and beckoned for another, arming himself for the inevitable, but needless, encounter with the host. At least the slave would make it in good time, before his father could reach him. Pollio Atticus, an influential senator and soon to be candidate for a consulship, laughed, smiled, shook hands and nodded in appreciation and agreement with any and all of his guests as he made his way through the crowd. Despite his silver hair and wrinkle-filled face, Pollio Atticus still possessed an air of vigour and virility (he still bedded two different women a week, neither of which were his wife). The "Augur", as he was titled in certain circles (for knowing – and shaping – which way the political wind would blow), was a man to be courted rather than crossed. He was "corrupt and corrupting" as Atticus had once explained to Maximus. The well groomed statesman was a man used to getting his own way, either through charm or more forceful means. Pollio Atticus was ever conscious of being in command of himself – and of those around him. He was man used to being listened to – and obeyed. Despite his will to dominate, the senator never displayed anger, or any unseemly emotion, in public. "I get even, rather than angry," he would icily state. Many a guest at the party could testify to the extent of how the would-be consul could ruin a rival both politically and financially. "He is Crassus, Seneca and Agrippina all rolled into one," one guest could be heard to whisper, in either admiration or condemnation, during the party.

"Evening. Claudia, would you be a dear and go see your mother? She wants to introduce you to someone, Marcus Dio," Pollio Atticus remarked warmly.

Claudia clasped her brother on the arm and smiled.

"Duty calls," she said to him, suspecting that the "someone" would be a person of influence who her father wanted her to seduce "in the interests of the family," as he often explained.

"Seems you may be about to die of boredom at this party too. Take care."

"Do visit before you leave Rome."

"I will," Atticus replied, offering his sister a reassuring smile – letting her know that he would indeed visit her and that he would be fine in dealing with their father. Claudia hugged her brother one last time, kissed him on the cheek and moved off in the direction of her mother – before her father could offer her a reproving look for keeping his guest waiting too long.

"I'm pleased that you could attend the party this evening, Rufus. It must have been a struggle to tear yourself away from another night in the barracks. At least the company is a tad more civilised here," Pollio Atticus said, offering his son a quick, sharp smile like a snake darting out his tongue.

"More civilised perhaps, but not necessarily more enjoyable – or honest."

For all intents and purposes it looked as though the father and son were engaged in polite conversation as they each nodded and smiled at one another. But years of mutual antagonism, bitterness and disapproval festered in every sentence spoken by the two men. Atticus had defied his father by joining the army. At first the statesman believed that his son would come crawling back to him, after experiencing the realities of the service. But his son proved him wrong and continued to defy him, crimes which Pollio Atticus refused to forgive. The two men had barely spoken a word to each other in the past five years.

"Your mother tells me that you are venturing off to the front again. Do you not think that it's about time you gave up this nonsense of playing the soldier? I still can't quite figure it out. Are you being stubborn? Is it because you think that women like a man in uniform? I can say with some authority that they also like a man in power. I shall laugh if you try to tell me that you have served this long out of a sense of duty. The Rufus Atticus I know has only ever had a sense of duty towards himself," Pollio Atticus derisorily remarked and laughed, whilst his eyes flitted about behind his son, checking to make sure that his guests were being attended to and to see if anyone else of importance had arrived.

The soldier's laughter was louder – and genuine – as he replied however, "Is the great Pollio Atticus attempting now to warn of the dangers of being selfish? I should inform all the lexicologists working in the libraries at Athens and Alexandria. I have discovered a new definition of irony. I'm pleased to say also that the Rufus Atticus you know is not the one I'm familiar with."

"Well, should you enjoy irony, you may be interested to know, believe it or not, that I partly arranged this gathering for your benefit. You should make some connections here. You still have the time and opportunity to make something of yourself and venture into politics."

"I'm not quite sure that those two things are as strongly related to one another as you might think."

Pollio Atticus made a sound – somewhere between a snort of contempt and an exasperated sigh. His son had been his greatest failure, when he had hoped that he would be his greatest success.

"There is a storm coming Rufus. The plague, the war with the Marcomanni and the rise in numbers of Christian dissidents – all these problems demand strong leadership, leadership which Aurelius is not providing. The people are scared and resentful. They want someone to cure our society's ills. Cornelius Sulla was right today to call for a larger, more powerful army. I will back his proposals."

"Is it not rather the case that he is backing your proposals? Aren't you a little too old to be getting into bed with Sulla? I didn't think you were his type," Atticus wryly replied, smiling into his wine. He soon gazed at his father with a sense of wariness and sobriety though, over the rim of the cup. He knew that his father also had investments in tin mines and with other military contractors, but was far more concerned with power than money. He had even been willing to prostitute his own wife in the past – as was doing now with his daughter – to win influence. How serious had he been in predicting, or providing, opposition to the Emperor? How much did he know his father – and what he was capable of?

The music stopped. Rain spotted the air. The women were the first to retreat inside, holding their hands over their various hairstyles, attempting to keep them dry. The men followed them into the large triclinium, which looked out onto the garden. Several of the guests wondered why their host and his son remained outside, still in conversation, in the ever worsening shower.

Pollio Atticus shook his head and screwed up his face, looking at his son as if he were further estranged, or disowned.

"Your jokes won't save Rome, Rufus. A powerful army will, which can be kept on a leash but set loose accordingly by its master. You are about to head off to the frontline, but you may find yourself involved in a different type of conflict soon. And, as with any fight, you will have to choose a side."

Pollio Atticus' tone sounded as ominous as the thunderous night sky. He may have lost his son's love over the years, but he hoped that Rufus was still wise enough to fear him. Anyone who was not an ally he would look upon as an enemy. Politics eclipsed life.

"I've already chosen," Atticus replied – and walked off to join the rest of the party inside.

7.

Maximus drained his cup of wine and re-filled it, again. Some people drink to feel alive. Maximus drank to deaden himself, to forget. He stared into the writhing flames of the fire, his expression as cold and fixed as the bust of Aristotle which Arrian kept in the triclinium. He remained seated and staring into the fire even when he heard the young German come up beside him.

"I couldn't sleep," Arrian remarked tiredly, wincing in discomfort slightly from his wound as he sat across from the centurion.

"Wine?"

Arrian shook his head. It was either too late, or too early, to start drinking. Although the adolescent would have an occasional cup of a fine vintage with his dinner, wine didn't agree with him.

"I'm not a big wine drinker."

"Well you might have to get used to the taste of it soon if we stay on the frontline in the north. Wine – and cheap wine at that – is often all there is to drink. Acetum lubricates the army."

"Germans love their wine too. I'm an exception that doesn't disprove the rule. I'm also an exception that doesn't disprove the rule in regards to my people being a warrior race. War is in their blood, as much as wine. I'm not sure I'll ever live up to my people though. You cannot put in what the gods have left out. This conflict could last for years. The wines will become vintages by the end. I can only see war, not peace," Arrian remarked, wincing now at the thought of the suffering the conflict would cause on both sides.

"Rome demands victory, not peace. You are a student of our history. Whether it be a contest against the

Carthaginians, Pyrrhus, the Persians or the Marcomanni, Rome will endure and will not stop until it's defeated its enemy."

"The irony is I believe that this war has been caused by our similarities rather than differences. I am not the only German who aspires to be more Roman than barbarian. Trade – and cultural exchanges – have brought our two peoples together over the past decades. We have grown as a civilisation, to such an extent that the northern tribes now want to be considered as an equal rather than as an inferior. Rome has wanted my people to be prosperous, but not too prosperous it seems; to be armed – and able to defeat Rome's enemies – but not too powerful. We want to grow economically, within a free market without trade restrictions and an oppressive bureaucracy. But Rome dictates the area of the free market. It sets unfair taxes and implements unfair subsidies. An autocratic political elite in Rome decides the fate of Germany – one which we have no power to elect in or vote out. And also, my people just want more living space."

Arrian made an impassioned argument, but Maximus remained impassive.

"Aye, so much so that they are willing to kill for it. But they will also die for it. The Marcomanni have sowed the wind. Now they must reap the whirlwind. They drew first blood, but we'll draw the last. Balomar must pay for his duplicity and war crimes."

The soldier drained his cup, again – sneering either at the sourness of the wine or at the mention of the German king. Yet Maximus had no desire to argue with his new young friend. He appreciated Arrian trying to defend his people, but rather than debate the causes of the war the soldier wanted to discuss how Rome could win it. The student shared his thoughts – feeling slightly conflicted as he did so as if he were betraying his homeland. Yet he also realised how, ultimately, he believed in the character and cause of Marcus Aurelius over the Marcomanni.

"...There is no capital to sack or pour salt into the soil of in the north. There is also no Hannibal to defeat with a single pitched battle to fight and win the war. If you cut off Balomar's head then, Hydra-like, two may grow in its place... We possess few archers and also swords, but every German is practised in using his spear... The warriors of the Marcomanni and other tribes will lack the discipline of the legions, but they do not lack courage or honour. Indeed be it through pride, or stupidity, the warriors will look to break the Roman line in the centre where it appears strongest... Our women can and will fight too."

"Atticus mentioned this. He also said that we should consider sending Roman wives and mother-in-laws to the front – so that they can nag our opponents to death." Rather than smiling though Maximus frowned, as he remembered Julia again. She would have laughed at the joke and enjoyed Atticus' company, he thought. He missed her laughter so much. He still occasionally woke and expected his wife to be next to him, his two children to be sleeping in the next room. Those few mistaken moments were the best part of his day – and the rest of his day was the worst part. Maximus drained his cup once more, hoping to wash away the painful, seductive memories – Siren songs.

The flames ceased to writhe, as if it they were too fatigued to do so. The wine became medicinal and helped the soldier drift off to sleep.

8.

"Romans may well know how to construct straight, flat roads but their ability to engineer carriages with effective suspension is somewhat lacking," a pinch-faced Galen expressed, unable to hear himself think over the loud rattle of the coach as it travelled along the road to Aquileia.

Accompanying the physician in the coach were Arrian and Aurelia. Galen added, "Apparently this coach once belonged to Lucius Verus. I'm surprised that the curtains were not permanently set to being drawn across, given his love of travelling with actresses – whose talents were far more apparent off stage I warrant. If Verus did previously use the coach to escort his mistresses across the empire then that would explain the well worn suspension."

Arrian covered his mouth with his hand and grinned, either at the physician's joke or at his priggishness.

"Would you like another cushion?" Aurelia remarked, kindly removing one of her own pillows from behind her back.

"No, my dear. But thank you. I will just duly suffer in silence," Galen stoically replied.

Arrian's grin widened and he shared a look with his sister. The good, fusty doctor had barely stopped complaining ever since they had left the capital. The landscape was featureless and colourless compared to the area surrounding his home in Pergamum. The language of the small attachments of legionaries guarding the party was as filthy as a sewer. And if the lunch he had was pork, he wanted the chicken. And if it was chicken, he wanted the pork.

It was not before long that the physician sighed in exasperation again – and his head came up from peering behind a book, which he could scarce read due to the jarring

22.

The wooden bridge bowed a little as the first of the enemy commenced to cross over it. Aurelius and Maximus looked down upon the scene – and felt the ground murmur a little. It dawned on the Emperor how a few hundred Romans would soon face a few thousand barbarians. The bulk of his army was still half a day away, at best. Maximus had inserted into the orders to the commanding officers of the legions that there was plunder to be had from the enemy. "That should put more of a spring in their step in them getting them to the party on time."

The ragged line of men snaking out from the woods, onto the road and then narrowing to cross the bridge seemed endless to Aurelius. It was a river of men – that his forces could drown in. His doubts began to re-surface and he already had the expression of a man in mourning, as if honouring the dead already.

"Are you sure that we should not wait for the rest of the legions?"

"I'm sure," the praetorian replied, squinting to see who appeared to be commanding the Marcomanni army. Was it Balomar himself? Had the Arivisto had time to join with their new allies? He then turned his attention back to his Emperor. "I remember you once giving Commodus some advice. You were in the garden. It was after one of his lessons. You said that one should not waste time arguing about what a good man should be, but rather be one. You should not now think too much on how a good commander should act, but rather be one."

Maximus fleetingly thought of the Emperor's son, how a wise man's advice would likely be in vain. Commodus was over-privileged, conceited and, though young, already developing a cruel streak. "The apple that fell from the tree seems to have landed in a different orchard," Atticus had once slyly quipped.

"I should have you writing philosophy, as well as commanding my armies, Maximus. You are right though. The God of War hates those who hesitate, as Euripides once wrote. Order the men to form up. We will advance down onto the plain. The enemy will look to stab through our shield walls with a column, but we will hold the line and cut off the head of the snake. Instruct what little number of archers we have to conceal themselves in the tree line – and attack the column from the side. Have one of the veteran cohorts join them. After blunting their frontal offensive we can attack their flank."

"And drive the bastards into the Danube," Maximus said, finishing off his Emperor's thought, if not quite using the language that he would have employed. "Hopefully the enemy will underestimate us and not commit all of their forces. Crossing back over the bridge will also delay any reinforcements. If we're lucky they'll also charge our lines early. The muddy ground will slow their momentum and sap their energy. But no matter what, our soldiers will stand."

"Because they'll fight for Rome?" the Emperor asked, his expression still creased in worry as he watched the line of enemy warriors continue to stream out of the forest.

"No. Because they'll fight for you."

*

"Are you nervous lad? You wouldn't be alone if you are," Atticus remarked. The optio noticed how Apollo's hands trembled as he sharpened his arrowheads one last time. It dawned on him also just how young the new recruit looked – and was. He still possessed puppy fat. Years of drink, violence and privation had yet to age his features like other legionaries. Atticus had seen twenty-five year olds with grey hair and the vacant stares of fifty year old veterans.

movements of the carriage. Unable to work, he turned his attention to his travelling companions.

"So, tell me, are you both looking forward to returning to your homeland?"

"I call Rome my home now. My village may well seem strange or backward should I go there. And we will appear alien to the tribe," Arrian replied, wistfully gazing out of the window, thinking more about what he was leaving behind rather than travelling towards. He missed his studies, books, the theatre and his tutors.

"And what about you Aurelia? Has Rome captured your heart like young Arrian here? Are you glad the Emperor has summoned you back to the north?"

"I love and respect my brother – and I am glad that he feels at home in the capital. But he knows how I am far from enamoured with Rome. I am looking forward to seeing my father and my village again. I do not feel altogether comfortable however in being used by the Emperor to win his war. We are unwittingly on the side of the Roman army – an army which is married to the causes of death and destruction," the woman answered forthrightly, her head raised up high as if she were giving a formal speech – or sermon.

"And also one which executes Christians," the doctor posited.

The gimlet-eyed, knowing look which accompanied Galen's statement probed as much as any of the physician's surgical instruments. Arrian crimsoned, as Aurelia blanched. Revealing his sister's secret could mean the death of both of them, Arrian worried. Indeed Galen's words hammered into him like nails upon a crucifix. The shock was akin to being stabbed again. Was Marcus Aurelius' physician merely fishing, or did he know Aurelia served a different god to that of the divine Emperor? Arrian's glance towards his sister contained a plea to let Galen's words pass, but her expression was already imbued with pride and defiance. She did not want to dishonour so many fallen martyrs who had suffered under Nero and other tyrants by denying her faith.

"How did you know?" Aurelia asked.

"I am a scientist. I come to evidence-based conclusions," Galen answered, matter-of-factly. Over the course of attending to her brother he had observed the woman reading certain books, heard her quote from certain texts in her conversation. She paraphrased Paul as much as her brother paraphrased Aristotle. She had also, on more than one occasion, passionately condemned the Empire's treatment of Christians too.

"I cannot, nor will not, renounce my Christian faith."

The carriage jolted up and down once more and Arrian felt like his sister's declaration had hammered another nail into his being. Many in Rome despised Christians more than Germans. They blamed the superstitious cult for all manner of ills – the plague, bad harvests and even rainy days. The new religion, which believed in one god (as opposed to the plethora of Roman, pagan gods) was also politically divisive. One's service to God should be sovereign over the service one owed to Rome and Caesar. For years the unofficial policy had been not to hunt Christians down and persecute them. Only those who became too militant – and who did not renounce their belief – were punished. But hostilities had grown towards the cult under the rule of Marcus Aurelius, an Emperor who was, ironically, lauded for his sense of tolerance and forgiveness. But the traditions, laws, religion and social institutions of the Empire were in direct conflict with Christianity. The Emperor was as much at war with an ideology as he was with the Marcomanni. Romans, Greeks, barbarians and Jews derided Christians – denouncing and attacking them. The appetite for persecuting Christians was as great as it had ever been – and as a result the lions in the arena had been well fed.

"Her belief is of a private rather than public nature now. She no longer sees her congregation even," Arrian said quickly to defend his sister – and mark her out as not being an enemy of the state. Aurelia stared at her brother with a storm in her eyes, but Galen spoke before she could reply how she no longer saw her congregation because the Praetorian Guard had arrested and executed them.

"Your secret is safe with me, do not worry. My job is to cure people, not send them to their deaths. Albeit you wouldn't think that all the doctors in Rome could claim to do no harm. The thoughtless quacks! But I am fine with you practising any religion you wish, just so long as you do no harm whilst doing so. People have often tried to pin certain beliefs on me. I've been called a stoic, empiricist, logician and all manner of things. The only being I see worth wholeheartedly believing in is myself however. I'm a Galenist. I'm jesting of course."

Arrian smiled in relief, rather than at the physician's joke. He concluded that doctor would not betray his sister's confidence. It was as if she were his patient – and indeed the philosophy student sometimes believed that Christianity was an illness that needed to be cured when it came to Aurelia. Christianity was as irrational as paganism. One should only have faith in scepticism, he reasoned. Arrian had hoped that it was just her congregation who were infecting her with the religion in the past, but her commitment and devotion waned not after their demise. If anything it increased. But as much as Arrian could have argued that his sister's faith now stemmed from a form of pride or conceit, he also knew that it brought a genuine sense of consolation and purpose to her life.

"Thank you for your understanding and discretion," Aurelia remarked. She squeezed the doctor's hand and smiled, gratefully, sweetly. Her aspect hardened again however as she mentioned how saddening it was that his friend, the Emperor, could not similarly be as tolerant and enlightened.

"Do not be too harsh on the Emperor, my dear. Marcus Aurelius is far more tolerant and enlightened than you give him credit for. Indeed he is the best man I know. You may now laugh at this, but he is in some ways the most Christian man I know also. Please do not let his views on religion colour everything you see. I dare say Marcus can appreciate how spiritually nourishing your beliefs are, but politically they may be considered poisonous. People who believe in a spiritual world still have to live in the real world too... Not all Christians are terribly Christian. They desire a vengeful rather than merciful God. They even applaud the plague – and see it as God's way of punishing Rome for its sins. Some are political, rather than divine, souls; self-interested revolutionaries, who crave a holy war. Aye, I have encountered many a Christian over the years Aurelia – and too many of them proved to be over zealous, overbearing and under sexed."

Aurelia appeared thoughtful and morose – recognising the wisdom in some of the things Galen had said.

*

Fingers of sunlight poked down through the ambling flocks of clouds. Half a dozen legionaries marched behind the carriage whilst another two, accompanied by Maximus and Atticus on their horses, walked in front of it. The road was flanked on both sides by woodland. Previously they had passed through farmland – which had appeared barren in contrast to when Maximus had last ventured north. The land needed to be tended to – but farmhands had been conscripted into the army during Rome's last recruitment drive.

Maximus patted and stroked the neck of his sorrel mare, in order to soothe the creature whilst a host of insects buzzed around its ears, and continued his discussion with his friend.

"Unfortunately any accusation made against your father will probably fall on deaf ears, or land you in trouble. He will be able to refute any allegation against him – it'll be your word against his. You'll be painted as a wilful son, trying to get revenge on his father for a personal slight. Your father has been a faithful servant of Rome over the years, as much as it now seems that he would like Rome to serve him. Hopefully we will have nothing to worry about. Ever since I've served in the army Rome has always had some form of a conspiracy or prospective coup that the gossip mongers have chewed upon. It may well have been that your father was just trying to reach out to you, attempt a reconciliation."

"In my experience the only thing that my father reaches out to is power. But perhaps I should give him the benefit of the doubt," Atticus replied, not entirely doubting his suspicions. But he was willing to change the subject. "I couldn't help but notice how my sister looked to reach out to you, so to speak, during our parting at the city gates. Claudia embraced you for so long that I thought you may have both been modelling for a sculptor. She seemed to whisper something in your ear too."

"You'll start to see conspiracies in the way the wind blows or in the cawing of crows soon. Your sister just asked me to look after you. She also invited me to dinner when we return to Rome, though the gods only know when that will be."

"Hmm, I certainly don't need the cawing of any crows to tell me that my sister would love to take advantage of you. I may well have to look after you at that dinner," Atticus said with a smirk and shake of his head, thinking of his wilful – and wily – sister.

"Claudia will have to get in the queue. The army and tax man already take advantage of me – although I'm all for her trying to get to my heart through my stomach."

"If I know my sister, it won't be your heart that she'll look to get to – but rather a different part of your anatomy."

The two friends shared a good humoured look and would have laughed together – but for the ambush.

9.

Men and horses appeared from out of the forest on both sides, like ghosts, with barely a broken branch or rustle of leaves. The bandits were well armed and well trained. The small group of legionaries behind the coach quickly snapped into a defensive position but they were equally quickly surrounded by a superior number of brigands, each carrying a spear or sword and small round shield.

Maximus and Atticus found themselves similarly outnumbered. Half a dozen bandits had run out from the tree line, accompanied by a trio of horsemen. The arrowheads, glinting in the sunlight, aimed at their chests, and checked any impulse the centurion and optio might have had to attack. A couple of the bandits behind the carriage howled in triumph and expectation.

Maximus remained calm and took in the scene and strength of the enemy. He then turned his attention to the leader of the group of brigands. The head of the gang sat upon a black cavalry charger in front of the officer. He was dressed in a bright blue tunic with yellow trim, over which he wore an ornate silver breastplate. His ears, fingers and neck dripped with gold jewellery, no doubt fruits of his labour from previous robberies. He was tall, wiry and looked as he if came from Spain or North Africa. Black, oily hair ran down past his shoulders. A smile, revealing a set of sharp yellow teeth, came out from beneath a well-kept forked beard. The two men, positioned either side of him on horseback, relaxed their bow arms – but still sat ready to release their shafts into the centurion and optio should the order be given.

"I am Sextus Bulla, you may have heard of me. My name should have sounded all the way back to Rome by now," the leader remarked, speaking in a charming tone, as if they were all at a dinner party.

"Rome may have problems hearing your name over the sound of your loud dress sense," Atticus drily replied.

Although Atticus pretended not to he had indeed heard of the brigand. He headed up one of a number of criminal gangs who terrorised the arteries of the Empire. They targeted wealthy travellers and merchants. In order to win the affection and loyalty of the regions they operated in, the thieves would share part of their spoils with the local people. He had been nicknamed "The Gentleman Bandit," due to his reputation for high fashion and good manners. But as well as wearing gold on his fingers Sextus Bulla had blood on his hands. His gang robbed, raped and murdered on a weekly basis. They also extorted as much money out of small businesses as the tax collector (well maybe not quite that much). The gang was also renowned for recruiting deserters to its lawless campaigns. They would escape from the armies serving along the Danube and Bulla would welcome them with open arms.

"You will do well to keep your jokes to yourself, unless you want to die laughing," the bandit replied. The mask of charm slipped from his face and Bulla spoke in a more guttural accent, but he soon regained his composure. "My quarrel is not with you centurion. We just want to unburden your carriage of its valuables and those passengers we can ransom. This can all be over quickly and painlessly – if you cooperate," Bulla said and nodded to a brace of men nearby him, instructing them to check out the carriage.

The two men ordered the passengers to get out of the carriage. They licked their lips and leered at Aurelia as she did so. Sextus Bulla smiled in satisfaction too.

"Don't worry. Everything will be fine," Maximus turned and remarked to the brother and sister as they huddled together, after being man-handled by their captors. For once Galen was short of something to say. He was used to metaphorical knives being drawn against him. They all looked scared and for once even Maximus appeared a little anxious.

"You're probably now thinking about playing the hero, but at best you'd be a tragic one praetorian. My men are well trained. Indeed you may have even been responsible for training some of them yourself. They're former legionaries. They grew tired of having empty bellies and empty purses. They also grew tired of serving under sadistic centurions and optios – and wouldn't think twice about killing an officer in cold blood. I hope you're not a sadistic officer of that ilk."

"Hopefully you'll soon get the chance to find out how sadistic I am," the centurion replied.

"Ha! I admire your spirit. But I'm still content to let you and your soldiers continue on your journey. If nothing else you can all go back to Rome and tell a story about how you encountered Sextus Bulla and, how like Julius Caesar, he displayed clemency. I'll even let you keep the old man. But your valuables and the Germans will be staying with me. And a good German is a dead German after all, no?"

Maximus and Atticus shared a fleeting look. Both now realised how the ambush had not just been bad luck, for how could Bulla know that the travellers were German?

The centurion turned his head and pensively gazed out into the forest, as if pausing for thought before making his decision. He sighed, either in a spirit of despair or fatalism. Arrian and Aurelia clasped each other's hand and stared at the officer with a mixture of hope and forlornness – for even if he defied the bandit and refused to hand them over, it was unlikely that the troops could defeat the enemy. The praetorian would give in to the brigand's favourable terms and spare his men. Rome looked after its own, Aurelia thought.

Maximus gave a nod of his head, as if assenting to the bandit's offer. For half a second Aurelia's heart sank and she cursed the centurion – and Rome – under her breath. She remembered what she had said to Julia, that "all soldiers were the same."

Bulla fingered one of his gold chains and grinned in triumph. All had gone to plan. He may have even permitted himself to laugh – but for the ambush.

10.

The arrow flew in at an angle from the treeline, but struck Bulla between his shoulder blades. The bandit let out a breathless scream as it punctured his lung. A few other arrows zipped in, striking either horses or men. The centurion had ordered a quartet of legionaries, who were skilled with a bow, to retreat into the woods and screen the party as soon as they had entered bandit country. Maximus had waited until his men were in position before giving the order to attack. Everyone froze in shock and confusion, except Maximus and Atticus. Before the brigand slumped forward and fell from his charger the optio drew his knives and took out the threat of the two archers on horseback in front of him. He then drew his sword and waded in to the enemy standing nearest to him, ordering the two legionaries behind him to do so also.

Maximus quickly wheeled his horse around and charged the two bandits who were guarding the Germans. One of the men had pulled his arm back and was about to stab Arrian, as he pushed himself in front of his sister. Before the enemy could strike, however, Maximus slashed him across the face with his gladius, whilst mowing his comrade down with his horse. The blood-curdling scream from the wounded bandit was soon silenced as the centurion plunged his sword through his upper chest. Blood spat through the air.

"Go back into the carriage. Arrian, pick up that sword. If anyone attempts to get inside then call out for help – whilst stabbing the bastards. Understand?"

The youth nodded, though understanding his task and being able to carry it out were two separate things.

The sound of arrows continued to hiss through the air behind him. The familiar noises of battle cries, death rattles and swords crashing onto shields also swirled around the praetorian. Maximus felt alive again, at home. He'd been organising the guard rotations at the imperial palace for far too long. He noticed how the legionaries behind the coach had put themselves on the front foot even without his orders. They moved towards the enemy in two well-disciplined lines with their shields up and spears pointing outwards. The intimidating sight caused a number of the enemy to return to type and desert. A group of brigands were starting to form their own line on one side of the road though, which would be long enough to wrap around his soldiers and perhaps encircle them. Maximus decided to even out the odds. He kicked his heels into his horse and attacked his enemy's flank, hacking away at the line of bandits as if he were a forester cutting a path through the woodland. Seeing the line in disarray the legionaries broke formation, launched their javelins and then ran to engage the enemy with their swords.

The sight of blood soon accompanied the familiar sounds of battle. Gore smeared their tunics and skin. A few of the enemy were able to retreat back into the forest, but most were put to the sword. Once the skirmish was over Maximus returned to the coach. He shared a look with his optio and friend which communicated gratitude, relief and praise. Atticus was helping a still shaken Aurelia down from the carriage, as Galen and Arrian stood beside him. The woman looked up at the centurion, her face pale and her lips still quivering. Tears, either of gratitude or despair, welled in her almond-shaped eyes. Maximus removed his cloak and placed it around her shoulders, smiling in a comforting manner as he did so. He then tenderly cupped his hand upon her arm. She didn't recoil – indeed she missed the sensation once the touch was gone. She wanted to say thank you – for saving her again – but was somehow unable to do so. Her usual icy expression melted away though – and Aurelia remembered her friend's reply, when she had condemned all soldiers: "No, he's different."

Maximus took the physician aside and asked if he could give the woman something to calm her nerves or help her sleep.

"I also want you to try and save that bastard Bulla over there, so I can torture him," the officer said. But even Galen failed to find a pulse. Maximus shot out a curse at hearing of the bandit leader's death, frustrated that he would not be able to find out any answers as to who had ordered the attack. He soon regained his composure though and asked Galen to attend to any injured legionaries.

Whilst Galen saw to the wounded Maximus went around and thanked and praised each soldier personally for the manner in which they had conducted themselves during the attack. The centurion took additional time out for the young legionary who had fired the arrow that had brought down the leader of the gang. The soldier was barely much older than Arrian. His brown hair was cropped short and there was an impish gleam in his expression. His bow and kit were in good order and his broad chest was puffed out, pleased and proud to be commended by his officer.

"That was a fine shot earlier. Was it a lucky one too? The best answer is the honest one. I'll know you're lying before you do, soldier," Maximus asked, remembering with mixed fondness how his former centurions had spoken to him in such a way.

"The harder you practise the luckier you get," the legionary replied confidently.

Maximus paused in thought for a moment, trying to remember where he had heard the phrase before. It was a good, if unoriginal, answer.

"What's your name?"

"Cassius Bursus. But most of the men call me Apollo, Sir," he remarked, holding up his bow by way of an explanation.

"The rest doubtless call you something far less complimentary. But here, take this. Have a drink or three tonight to celebrate," the centurion said, retrieving a silver coin and tossing it to the fresh-faced recruit.

"Forgive me, Sir, but what am I supposed to be celebrating?" Apollo replied, squinting from both the light and in slight confusion.

"You've just joined the Praetorian Guard."

11.

The inn they stayed in that evening was much like any other. It met their needs but there was a lot left to be desired in regards to the establishment and its amenities. Most of the rooms were as filthy as the jokes the legionaries shared over dinner and the innkeeper had a list of extra charges that would have made even a quartermaster blush. But the wine wasn't watered-down (that much), the food was fresh-ish and most importantly the serving girls were willing to work overtime through the night, servicing the soldiers. A number of the girls worked overtime throughout dinner too, hoping to catch the eye of the attractive, well-spoken optio. But unfortunately for them – and him – Maximus had other plans for Atticus. In light of the attack that afternoon the centurion arranged for his optio to provide close protection for Arrian and Aurelia.

"There have been a couple of occasions when I've been in the same room as a husband and wife, hiding beneath the bed, but this will be the first time that I've been in the same room with a brother and sister," Atticus remarked to Maximus over the dinner table.

"Well you're always saying how much you crave new experiences, to help fight off boredom."

"I warrant that boredom may well prove victorious this evening still. I'm just pleased that you trust me enough to share a room with the woman."

"I don't trust you. But I do trust her. It could be worse. Young Apollo over there will be spending half the night posted outside the door of the room. Let's just hope that he's as attentive to his duties as he is to that brunette serving him up his main course."

"I'm not sure which he's salivating over more."

"I am," the centurion replied with a hint of a smile, remembering his days as a new recruit and enjoying the charms of serving girls who knew what they were doing in the kitchen – and bedroom.

"Shall we buy an hour or two of her time as a reward for his promotion?"

"He'll only need an hour, at most. I've just paid for his food and drinks for the evening though. You can his pay for the dessert."

*

A couple of extra braziers (which they would be charged extra for) lighted and heated the musty, low-ceilinged room. Arrian and Aurelia sat, leaning forward, perched upon two chairs, listening to the optio. Atticus encouraged his audience to have a measure or two of wine – at the very least, it would help them sleep he argued. After discussing the Parthian campaign, Arrian asked the optio why he had given up his studies to become a soldier. Was it not true that he was an accomplished poet in his youth?

"Soldiers make more money than poets. And women like a man in uniform," Atticus argued, winking at the German student as he did so. Arrian grinned, whilst Aurelia rolled her eyes. Rather than Atticus, Aurelia wanted to now know more about the optio's superior officer – and she steered the conversation towards the subject of Maximus accordingly.

"Your centurion displayed a great deal of courage today to fight for us. No one would have thought less of him I suspect if he would have handed over two Germans to save the lives of twenty Romans," Aurelia said, whilst watering down the wine some more.

"He would have thought less of himself," Atticus replied, inwardly sighing at the woman for turning wine into water. He also thought how Maximus sometimes acted as if the ghost of Julia was standing by him, as if he didn't want her to think less of him. The optio had only met his centurion's wife on a few occasions, but she still made a favourable impression. Atticus thought her intelligent, without being conceited; she was attractive, without being vain. She was not without cynicism, but more memorably she was not without compassion. Most of all he remembered how Julia, more than anyone else, could make Maximus laugh. She had the dry and black humour of a soldier, but still remained wonderfully sweet. As far as Atticus knew his centurion remained faithful to his wife whilst they were married. Atticus recalled how, drinking the night away after a winning an engagement against the Parthians, Maximus confessed to him that he was happy because he had been fortunate enough to marry his best friend.

The optio paused in his thoughts due to hearing increasingly audible sounds come from the neighbouring room. The bed began to knock against the wall. A woman's voice could be heard to impatiently utter, "Hurry up". Arrian appeared slightly embarrassed, Aurelia pursed her lips in disapproval and Atticus raised a corner of his mouth in a half-smile as he heard the soldier emit a groan (although he was unable to determine whether the groan was borne from fatigue, drunkenness or ecstasy).

*

The braziers murmured and half a dozen insects buzzed above her head. The bed was hard and rickety on the creaking floor. But there were other reasons why Aurelia was unable to drift off to sleep. She grieved for her friend, again. Julia had been a Christian and, for a time, Aurelia's closest companion. The two women had met by accident one afternoon, both finding shelter from the rain beneath the same awning in the market. They soon began to shop and attend the theatre together. They swapped recipes, as Aurelia improved her friend's culinary skills. In return Julia improved Aurelia in other ways. She introduced her to new people and also new authors, as they swapped not just cookery books – but plays, history books and philosophical texts. Aurelia made a leap of faith one evening and confessed her devotion to the Christian religion to her friend. Julia, curious about the religion and wishing to support her companion, attended a few gatherings. Although Julia was hesitant about wholly committing herself to joining Aurelia's congregation she found meaning and purpose in the Gospels. She started to believe. Aurelia wanted her friend to give more of herself however.

"You should marry yourself to God," she argued, brimming with religious fervour.

"But I already have a husband and as far as I know he doesn't want a divorce quite yet, despite my cooking," Julia replied, jokingly. But Aurelia failed to laugh at the comment.

"He is a soldier, part of Satan's army," Aurelia declared, quoting from a sermon that she had attended the previous week.

"Gaius is a good man. You'll see. I'd love you to have dinner with us both when he returns from the front." Julia was tempted to add how her husband was a better man than most in regards to those in the congregation, especially the religious scribes who failed to practice what they preached. They acted as though they were the key holders to the Kingdom of God. She was also tempted to say how much she worried that Aurelia was changing. She was losing her sense of humour and sense of perspective, being blinded by the teachings of her church – which were not always in harmony with the teachings of Christ.

When Maximus came back to Rome Julia spent less time with Aurelia. Aurelia grew resentful and jealous of the soldier – even though she had never met him – for stealing her best friend. At the time Aurelia felt increasingly isolated as her congregation discovered that she was the daughter of a German chieftain – and the war with the Marcomanni had commenced. People distanced themselves from her. *Not all Christians are terribly Christian.*

Aurelia confronted her friend after the praetorians arrested a number of worshipers in her congregation. The charge was that they had been conspiring against the state. She called Maximus the enemy and urged Julia to leave him. She told her how the soldier had been present at the trial and execution of their friends, although she was only sure that he had been in attendance at the former.

"In the same way that Man cannot serve both God and Mammon, you cannot serve God whilst being married to such a sinner."

"I love my husband," Julia had replied, with a gentleness and wisdom that was in stark contrast to the ire of her shrill friend. They were the last words that Aurelia ever heard her say. Shortly after their argument Julia and her children fell ill. Aurelia wanted to visit the house, to help in any way she could. But she didn't. She wanted to apologise. But she didn't.

Tears glistened in Aurelia's eyes as she lay upon her side and curled up in a ball on the bed. The feelings of guilt and grief which knotted her stomach were as palpable as the feelings of hunger in a beggar. She silently prayed to God for strength and forgiveness – again – and tried to take some consolation from Julia being in a better place.

"I love my husband."

Aurelia recalled her friend's words once more and for the first time could appreciate why she had said them. *Perhaps he is a good man.*

12.

The afternoon sun burnt through the clouds like wax. Sweat glazed the limbs of the marching legionaries. The party would reach Aquileia by nightfall.

The autumnal russets and browns of the north had replaced the vernal greens of Italy. The forests were denser and pungent with the smell of peaty soil, verdure and swampland. Trees – oaks, ferns, willows and birches – towered over them. Shrubs, mushrooms and blackberries sprouted up everywhere. Occasionally one could hear the distant howl of a wolf, or the rough snort of a wild-boar. All manner of birdsong, entwined like myrtle, whistled out from the trees. Yet as they grew closer to the front and the wilds of his homeland Arrian saw evidence of civilisation increase rather than diminish. Instead of the muddy tracks and wattle and daub dwellings he remembered from childhood, he saw now Roman-built stone houses and forts. Wide all-weather roads serviced soldiers, local people and tradesman alike.

Arrian had claimed a bandit's horse. He rode up alongside Maximus and his optio. He rode uneasily, shifting uncomfortably in the saddle and out of tune with the rhythms of his mount. Muscles ached that, before the morning, the student scarce knew he possessed. Atticus had put him through his paces that morning, in terms of a conditioning and fencing session. Having felt so helpless during the attack on his house – and the carriage – Arrian asked Maximus if he could give him some rudimentary training so as to be able to defend himself – and his sister – should they be put in peril again. The centurion admired the young man's intentions, if not his abilities, and asked his optio to commence the training sessions. It was perhaps out of a sense of amusement, rather than duty, that Atticus spent so long with the German. Arrian had to constantly pause to catch his breath – and Atticus had known blind men who could wield a gladius more effectively.

"So do you think that we will see the Emperor late this evening or tomorrow?" Arrian asked, nervous and excited about meeting with the revered Marcus Aurelius.

"Probably. Our Caesar is a night owl rather than a lark," Maximus answered.

"How well do you know the Emperor? What's he like?" Arrian posed, leaning forward, eager to hear the reply and trying to find a more comfortable position on his horse.

The centurion thought how he knew the Emperor more than most, but at the same time he barely knew him at all. Thankfully Aurelius was more a son of Pius than Hadrian. Traits such as rapaciousness, paranoia, cruelty, depravity and weak-mindedness filled out the history books in regards to describing past Emperors – but a young Aurelius had studied history in order to try to avoid repeating the mistakes of others. At the same time as there being a constancy and equanimity to his temper, Aurelius once confessed to Maximus that he sometimes felt like a walking contradiction – with the duties and mind-sets of being both an Emperor and a philosopher pulling him in opposing directions. The centurion recalled how, late one night, shortly after hearing about the Marcomanni's incursion across the Danube, Aurelius had buried his head in his hands and confessed, "If I wasn't so worried about being succeeded by a Nero or Tiberius I would be tempted to abdicate and spend the rest of my days studying. But, as you know only too well Maximus, duty calls – and it shouts so loudly sometimes that we cannot turn a deaf ear to the sound... To find peace may be considered to be the aim of a philosopher, but as Emperor I must go to war..."

Despite considering himself a walking contradiction Maximus believed that Aurelius had found a balance, harmony, in his soul. He was content in his sorrow, as though melancholy was the apogee of wisdom; if Aurelius didn't feel sorrowful then he was somehow not being true to himself. Similarly Maximus often believed that if he was somehow not feeling grief then he was not being true to himself, or Julia.

But sorrow seldom turned into bitterness or enmity. Maximus had never known the Emperor to raise his voice, lose his temper or allow his passions to overrule his judgement. Many criticised the Emperor behind his back for his lack of warmth or affection, but for Maximus it was far more important that Aurelius was never cold or vindictive. He just sometimes seemed detached from the world, as though the realm of abstract thought was the real world – to which he was a devoted citizen. Unlike many of his predecessors Aurelius did not lack a sense of modesty and humility either. He would cut short any flattery if ever he was unjustly (or justly) praised, or direct the praise onto another. For those who believed Aurelius lacked or warmth or affection, they should have heard him talk of his fondness and admiration for Antonius Pius.

"How well do I know the Emperor? Well enough."

Before the praetorian could say anything else he was distracted by the sight of Aurelia trotting towards him on Bulla's black charger. Unlike her brother she rode well, perfectly poised and in control whilst riding side saddle (albeit Aurelia wished she was dressed differently and able to sit astride her mount). She had, quite literally, let down her hair. Her glossy tresses blew as freely in the breeze as her horse's mane. There was a contented smile on her face and colour in her cheeks. Finally she's stopped trying to look like a Vestal Virgin, Atticus mused.

Maximus, his optio and even Arrian all remained stunned, their mouths slightly agape. Finally Aurelia broke the silence.

"I became bored with the conversation in the carriage. It consisted of Galen talking to himself – about himself."

There was good humour, rather than haughtiness, in her voice. The men all laughed – and even a couple of the horses whinnied, as if laughing too. Aurelia flicked her reins and rather than trot up beside her brother she positioned herself next to the still somewhat bewildered centurion. He gazed at the woman, his head slightly cocked, as if she were a stranger. Arrian recognised her however as his amiable and witty sister of old.

"Do you think that we will get to Aquileia before the end of the day?"

"I hope so. Atticus may well mutiny if not. He's never been this long without a fine vintage in front of him at dinner before," the centurion wryly replied, in earshot of his friend.

The optio smirked and thought how he was not only pining for a decent vintage.

"Abstinence does not make the heart grow fonder," Atticus remarked, thinking of how he was missing his dessert, as well as his wine, at dinner each night.

"And what do you think will happen to us once we reach the Emperor?" Aurelia asked – and then gently closed her eyes, letting the rays of the sun and a cool breeze wash over her skin.

"I suspect that he will ask you to carry on your journey, talk to your father – and petition for him to side with Rome against its enemies. Or at the very least remain neutral."

"And will you continue to act as our escort?"

"I'm not sure. I'll duly find out after I have spoken to the Emperor."

"I hope you will remain by our side. You never know, I may even make a request for you to accompany us," Aurelia said, smiling slightly after witnessing the soldier's startled reaction.

Atticus coughed, as the gulp of water went down the wrong whole in his throat on hearing Aurelia's comment and witnessing the light in her eyes. She could perhaps even teach Claudia a thing or two about flirting, the optio jokingly thought.

"And will you do so out of a sense of a reward, or punishment, for us?" Maximus queried, arching his eyebrows in amusement – and amazement.

"You will find out, after I have spoken to the Emperor," Aurelia answered, unable to suppress an attractive, unaffected grin. For the first time she looked upon the soldier as a potential friend rather than enemy and it felt good.

13.

"They can kill me, but they cannot hurt me," a tired looking Marcus Aurelius philosophically stated, as much to himself as to Maximus, in reply to the centurion's report. "The events in Rome and on your journey here do indeed add up to the sum of a conspiracy."

The room was modestly furnished, merely containing a desk and several bulging bookcases. A large map of the region also covered one whole wall in the room. The house was modest too. The governor of Aquileia had offered his Emperor the use of his own residence but Marcus Aurelius had replied that although he could accept the use of a man's house, he had no right to turf him out of his family home. The smaller villa that he chose to live in and work out of also possessed the virtue of not being able to accommodate an army of visitors, attendants and advisers. The most powerful man in the world wore a clean, plain tunic. His figure was devoid of jewellery. His hair and beard needed trimming. "I would much prefer to be Diogenes to Alexander the Great," the soldier had once heard his Emperor confess. Maximus had requested to see his commander-in-chief as soon as the party arrived at the town, to brief him on recent events. Aurelius admitted the praetorian immediately and calmly sat behind his desk as he listened to the centurion's revelations, showing little reaction and seldom interrupting the officer as he did so.

Maximus resisted telling his Emperor about Atticus' suspicions, in regards to his father, in his report. Not only did he not possess a shred of evidence to substantiate any accusation, but the centurion did not wish to further sour his optio's relationship with his father. Similarly, with one wrong word, he could jeopardise Atticus' future career prospects, whether they rested in the military or in politics.

Marcus Aurelius pursed his full, unsmiling lips. His deep set, dark eyes seemed to look through Maximus for a moment or two. But his expression soon softened and he even appeared to shrug his shoulders at the officer's ominous report.

"We should remain conscious of there being some sort of a conspiracy afoot, but as Galen might say we cannot come to any conclusions without any evidence. We cannot even deduce whether our antagonists are from Rome or the north, or elsewhere. Ironically they may have helped rather than hindered us. I am even more determined now to ask the brother and sister to intercede with their father and win his support – seeing as how much our enemies fear the Arivisto becoming an ally. No, I will not allow the shadow of a threat to alter my plans, nor will I spend precious time on speculating where this threat might come from. Any conjecture will prove as substantial as idle gossip. I warrant that I am as likely to encounter an assassin as I am a sober Briton."

A rare joke and a rare smile lit up the Emperor's careworn features. Maximus smiled at witnessing the light and humour back in the sorrowful man's eyes.

"We must look forward rather than backwards, Maximus. Thank you for your report, but let us not dwell upon things which are unknown or things we cannot alter. We need to look to the present and future, to a victory. I do not believe I lack moral courage, but I am still to be tested in regards to physical courage. I am a commander yet to lead his army in a battle."

An Emperor was supposed to be semi-divine, but Aurelius was here admitting how he was all too human – and Maximus admired his general all the more for it. Maximus would have given his life for the noble man – his friend – in front of him even if he were a goat herder, instead of a Caesar.

"I do not doubt your moral or physical courage – the former will fuel the latter when the time comes."

"Thank you, Gaius. Your faith in me may help alleviate my doubts, but unfortunately you not have the power to dissolve my anxieties completely. Being guilty of thinking too much as a legislator is no great crime, but as a military leader I must be bolder in my actions. A year ago people spoke of the fruits of victory, but I fear this army may be beginning to wither on the vine. You have already heard the rumours about the extent of the desertions and disease in our army. Unfortunately many of the rumours are true. I worry that I have let enemy forces slip through my fingers. When the soldiers of Rome witnessed the sight of Caesar's cloak billow in the air at Alesia it was said to be worth another two cohorts. Should the armies of Rome now see my cloak billow they would but merely conclude that it was a windy day.

"I have recently won certain diplomatic battles, by bribing a number of tribes to fight on our side or remain neutral. But this war cannot be won through diplomacy alone. My sword has yet to see sunlight, let alone taste blood. The end to this conflict seems further away now than it did a year ago. And all the while the capital is lacking an Emperor. I even miss pretending to watch and enjoy the games at the Coliseum, whilst I work through correspondence. Commodus is growing up without his father. My wife says she misses me, though I suspect that she would miss Rome – and its shoe shops – more if she were here, by my side. Faustina was displeased with me when I left for the front, for auctioning off some of our valuables to help finance the war. I sold a diamond brooch of hers, which she still hasn't forgiven me for. You could say that the incident caused the sparkle to go out of our marriage."

Aurelius sighed, either in woe or indifference. He looked up at the dutiful praetorian and saw a model of stoicism, gaining strength from him. Earlier in the week he had written, "*Be like a headland of rock on which the waves crash upon incessantly. But the rock stands fast and the seething waters eventually settle.*" Perhaps he had been unconsciously thinking of Maximus whilst composing the meditation, Aurelius mused.

"But rather than lament the absence of my wife, I should be grateful for the presence of yourself. It's good to see you Gaius," the Emperor declared, rising to his feet and fraternally squeezing the centurion's shoulder. This was not the first time that the Emperor had shared some of his private thoughts with the praetorian, or been grateful for him for completing a mission. "I dare say that it has something to do with your sword arm, as opposed to the hand of a god, in keeping you and your party safe – but let us give thanks to the gods all the same. And how is Atticus? I trust he is in good health too? Atticus is a world of possibilities; I just wonder whether he has settled upon which possibility he wants to realise. He is a talented poet, a keen student of philosophy. He is also an accomplished soldier – and could flourish in politics too. Yet as much as he often appears contented when I see him I believe him to be far from satisfied with his life. There is a hole in his soul."

"I told him the other week that he needed the love of a good woman – and that he should take a wife. He replied that he preferred to have the love of several women. And he also said that he has already taken a wife – but she's married to someone else."

"It seems that Atticus has changed about as much as the position of our frontline over the past year. My only historic achievement so far in this conflict is to do what no other man has ever come close to doing before – unite the German tribes, against a common enemy."

"You should not be so hard on yourself," Maximus said, worried to see his Emperor appear so vulnerable and defeatist.

"I have to be hard on myself. I'm the Emperor, no one else will dare say anything to my face. Except perhaps you would be honest and brave enough to do so, Gaius. Certainly there has been plenty of talk behind my back. The people expect and demand an early, favourable end to the war. I am given to understand that some of the graffiti back in the capital has been quite witty and imaginative. The Senate has also been justified in some of its veiled, or unveiled, criticisms."

"You cannot please all of the people all of the time, even when at peace. Seldom can war be waged without any reverses. As you once told me, the acclamations of the multitude are akin to just the clapping of tongues."

"Who am I to ignore the wisdom of an Emperor?" Aurelius replied, half-smiling all too wistfully and briefly. "But I could use your counsel now, Gaius. Help me win this war." These last words come out as more of a plea than command.

"In the same way that Caesar crossed the Rubicon you must cross the Danube to defeat the Marcomanni," Maximus said with determination, looking up at the large map upon the wall.

"Everywhere we've tried to cross we've been repulsed, or defeated. Various generals change their minds each day as to the best strategy. Where would you attack?"

The seasoned soldier drew his knife, studied the map intently for a few seconds, and plunged the blade into the wall as if he were stabbing the enemy itself.

"There. Pannonia... Sometimes you've just got to get into the fight."

14.

A silvery-grey haze, the colour of cobwebs, began to bleed into the night sky. Dawn would soon wash over Rome, as would a soupy brown acrid fog of smoke from furnaces, kilns, ovens and house fires. Pollio Atticus was in his study, his temper as hot as the coals burning in the braziers. His liver-spotted, claw-like hand screwed itself into a fist and he pounded the large cedar wood desk. Chen had just relayed the news from one of their agents that the attempted abduction of the Germans, by Bulla, had failed. This was now the second time that the brother and sister had slipped through the statesman's fingers. One of his agents had discovered that the Emperor had summoned for the children of the chief, in order to gain his support in the war. Pollio Atticus, to foil the Emperor's plans, had decided to abduct and murder the young Germans before they reached Aquileia. The chief of the Arivisto tribe would consequently withdraw any support for Aurelius. He may have also considered that blood was on the Emperor's hands and he would have sided with Balomar in the war. To add insult to injury it seemed that his own son had been instrumental in scuppering his plans.

"Damn Bulla, damn those half-wits from the tavern, damn Aurelius and damn my own son!"

The bust of Augustus shook as the senator continued to pound the desk. Spittle, along with motes of dust, peppered the air. Chen sneered in derision and sympathy, baring his sharp white teeth.

"At least the fool Bulla died in the ambush. Dead men tell no tales. Maximus and my son are no fools however – they may now consider that the original attack on the house wasn't a mere coincidence. Deal with that useless cretin

Sinius," Atticus snarled, his usually well-oiled hair now out of shape.

"Dead men tell no tales," the Chinese bodyguard replied, his sneer transforming itself into a sly grin. He already pictured slitting the man's throat, the polished blade of his ivory handled dagger glinting in the moonlight. He would duly give Sinius the opportunity to fight for his life and draw his blade too. His vain thrusts and appeals for mercy would amuse the sadistic assassin.

"We just have to hope that Aurelius proves to be the author of his own demise. Just one more defeat will turn the desertions into a full-blown mutiny. The Emperor has poetry in his heart – but Rome needs a leader with iron his soul."

Certain things are in place, the senator thought to himself with satisfaction. Significant members of the military and Senate had commenced a whispering campaign against the Emperor, doubting his suitability to lead Rome in such a crisis. They would raise their voices in earnest after one more setback. The likes of Cornelius Sulla and Marcus Dio were major players – and he could put words into their mouths at will. Atticus had the influence and money to put forward a candidate to fill the power vacuum, the commander Avidius Cassius. He had already secured the officer's loyalty – paying off his debts and promising him the hand of Claudia in marriage. She had duly bewitched Cassius, even before bedding him. But the wily senator had no desire to openly usurp the Emperor. He who wields the dagger never wears the crown. No, he would rather be a Sejanus than Tiberius – the power behind the throne. Pollio stepped forward out of the shadows when Pius had died and offered to mentor the inexperienced Aurelius – but the Emperor kept his own counsel. The senator retreated back into the shadows, nursing his wounded pride and will to revenge.

"Just one more defeat. And then I will make my bid for power. Vespasian, Claudius, Galba – soldiers crown Emperors, not gods. Our fates lie in ourselves, not in the stars. The Praetorian Guard will not even be able to protect Aurelius should the legions turn against him. Indeed the Praetorian Guard may turn against him first," Atticus remarked, smirking at the prospect. Yet thinking upon the famed regiment forced the senator to think again about his irksome son. If he could not win the loyalty of just one optio, who was his own blood, how could he hope to win over the entire Guard? If only Rufus knew how instructions had been given to Bulla to spare all the soldiers during the ambush. The smirk fell from the old man's face, his crabby countenance heavy with bitterness and grief.

As if second guessing his master's thoughts Chen remarked, "And what of your son? When the time comes – and if he chooses to stand between you and the Emperor – what would you like me to do?"

"He's dead to me already. It will be of no matter to kill him again."

15.

"We defy augury," Atticus playfully argued, quoting a line from his favourite tragedy, when replying to the woman in bed next to him. Sabina had just told the soldier of the dream she had during the night, in which she had seen Atticus die in the forests of the north. It still wasn't too late to find someone else to volunteer for the mission of taking the Germans north. He shouldn't tempt the fate of her dream, she argued. Sabina would be lonely without him. Atticus suspected that the insatiable merchant's wife would not miss him for too long. She doubtless had a man in every fort, but the optio didn't think less of her for it. He had also met the woman's husband – and could not wholly blame the young, alluring wife for her infidelities. Galen should bottle the merchant's conversation and sell it as a sleeping potion, Atticus joked.

Sabina hooked her slender legs around his, her almond-shaped eyes smiled in sultriness. Her hand reached down underneath the sheets.

"Well I don't want you defying me, Rufus Atticus. And I don't want some barbarian woman taking your heart either."

"I'm much more concerned about some barbarian woman taking my life," he countered.

"You shouldn't joke," she replied admonishingly, hitting him on the chest too as a further rebuke.

The soldier thought how he had little choice but to deal with things through a sense of humour. One either laughed along with the joke of life, or fell victim to one of its punch lines.

*

"How do you think father will react when he sees us?" Aurelia asked, as she and her brother packed their saddle bags for the journey ahead.

"He will likely greet you with a hug and me with a scowl or grunt. I think Maximus and the Emperor overestimate the influence I might be able to bring to bear. But I do not want to let them down," Arrian replied, recalling the last exchange of letters between himself and his father. His father had sent him a letter explaining how he had recently acknowledged his illegitimate son, Balloc – and that he had announced him to the tribe as his heir. Whilst Tarbus may have believed that he was punishing his son, Arrian had breathed a sigh of relief upon reading the news. He could continue his studies and be free from the responsibility of returning to the north. He would rather be the thousandth man in Rome, as opposed to the first man with the Arivisto.

"What did you and the Emperor speak about at dinner? He seemed glad to give you his ear at the end of the table."

"We talked about literature, history, philosophy. He is remarkably well read. He recommended some philosophy tutors I should call on when we return to Rome. And he said he would provide some letters of introduction." Arrian remembered again the Emperor's words at the end of the evening. The philosophy student had asked; if the Emperor could impart one piece of wisdom gleaned from his studies and life what would it be? Aurelius had paused briefly in thought, equally amused and intrigued by the question, before replying, "While thou livest, while thou mayest, become good."

Rain drummed across the roof. Arrian rolled his eyes, realising how he was truly back in his sodden homeland. He scrunched his face up in vexation as he held aloft the pair of uncomfortable woollen trousers he would have to wear. Dressing in a Roman tunic could get him killed, once he crossed the Danube.

"But tell me, what were you and Maximus talking about at dinner? The rain in our homeland seems to have washed away your animus towards him."

Arrian smiled, as he recalled Atticus' whispered comment over dinner – that his sister was batting her eyelids at Maximus so much he was worried that she might blow out the candles on the table. Aurelia blushed, either from the embarrassment at being reminded of her previous attitude towards the centurion, or from something deeper. She had told herself that she would make an effort with the praetorian for Julia's sake, but it was more than that now. She liked him, for her sake.

*

Galen finished taking the Emperor's pulse. The stoical doctor reacted with neither concern nor contentment in regards to the prognosis. The patient similarly remained impassive – and enquired not as to whether all was satisfactory. The two friends merely carried on their conversation. They sat under an awning in the garden of the Emperor's villa. The worst of the rain had passed it seemed, but drizzle still misted up the air.

"The mission will provide Maximus with a distraction from his grief. Should he encounter the enemy then he may well be granted that which he perhaps desires most – his death," Marcus Aurelius posited. Maximus was his first choice to escort the brother and sister through enemy territory back to the Arivisto tribe – even before the centurion volunteered for the task and Arrian and Aurelia requested his presence.

"I dare say that, in Rome, in protecting you or fighting for his comrades, Maximus has something to die for. I'd just prefer that he had something to live for too. Let us hope that the mission doesn't prove a suicidal one," Galen replied, watching a bird dart across his vision and wondering if he had encountered the species before.

"Maximus will not fail us. I cannot speak for Tarbus, the chief of the Arivisto, however. He could stand beside us like a lion, or his tribe could turn on us like a pack of wild dogs – smelling the blood of a weakened prey. Balomar may yet buy the support of the Arivisto before us also. My agents inform me that he has entered into the region, accompanied by a war chest to purchase loyalty and arms. The Marcomanni are growing in strength," the Emperor stated, sighing from a sense of tiredness or pessimism.

"You need to be mindful of your own strength, as well as worrying about the condition of your enemy. You need to sleep more and regain your appetite."

"I'll regain my appetite, my friend, once I've tasted victory."

*

Maximus spent most of the day on a run. He ran till his lungs burned and his feet bled, but still the centurion could not outrun his grief and memories. He might as well have tried to outrun his shadow. He remembered how he used to tell his son, Lucius, about his namesake: Lucius Oppius, the *Sword of Rome* – the standard bearer who led the invasion off the British coast. Oppius stood by Caesar as he crossed the Rubicon and fought at Pharsalus. He had also protected the young Octavius Caesar, as he travelled to Rome from Apollonia. Maximus pictured his son's face, bright-eyed and captivated by his stories. He tried his best to remember the sensation of Julia affectionately squeezing his hand. They held hands as if they were still teenage sweethearts, long after their wedding day. Foul as well as fond memories assaulted his thoughts though. Images of emaciated, sweat-glazed faces. A succession of funerals – for those who he lived for. Waking up in taverns, sick caked on his chin, from having drunk himself into oblivion, having been too frightened to go home to an empty house. Anger as well as sorrow swelled in his breast. Should a priest, or a God even, have tried to explain to him how the deaths of Lucius and

Aemelia were part of a greater plan then he would have drawn his sword and run them through.

Maximus also ruminated upon his impending mission as he pounded along the woodland tracks and through the mountain passes. Unfortunately the intelligence was scant as to the number of enemy between them and the Arivisto tribe. Similarly, they couldn't be sure of the welcome they would receive when, or if, they reached their destination. The mission was hazardous; but it was also potentially vital to the war effort. The centurion found himself thinking about Aurelia during his run too. He had enjoyed sitting next to her at dinner the previous evening. Maximus couldn't quite understand why the woman had softened towards him – he was just grateful for her apparent change of heart. He told himself that her new found amiability was welcome as it would make the coming mission easier, but maybe his gratitude was borne from something else.

*

When Maximus returned to camp he sought out Apollo. He found the young soldier in a tavern. The new recruit stood to attention when seeing his officer but the centurion told him to sit, bought him a drink and gave him a gift.

"I can't really compete with the present Atticus gave you to unwrap in the tavern last week but, here, take this," Maximus said, giving Apollo a finely crafted dagger. "Think of it as a thank you present."

"What are you thanking me for, Sir?"

"You're about to accept an important assignment."

Apollo immediately felt a rush of excitement and pride at being chosen to carry out a special mission, but when he took in the grave expression on his commanding officer's face the archer began to realise that promotion to the Praetorian Guard could be the death – rather than the making – of him.

16.

The small size of the party (Maximus, Atticus, Arrian and Aurelia) meant that it could wend its way through the country nimbly and largely undetected. When they did encounter enemy soldiers or civilians Maximus and Atticus were pleasantly surprised with the young German's confidence and resourcefulness in dealing with his countrymen. He declared that he was the son of the chief of the Arivisto, on his way back home to join his father to fight the Roman invaders, and that he had employed a brace of deserters as bodyguards.

"I must confess Arrian, I've been impressed by the way you've handled yourself when we've encountered the enemy. You've lied so well that you might want to consider a career in politics," Atticus amiably conveyed to the student as he trotted beside him. They were riding abreast along a woodland track. Spindly branches, like bony fingers, hung over them. Plaintive birdsong blew through the trees, as did the stench of a nearby marsh. The air was damp, presaging rain. Hooves sloshed in the mud.

"I warrant that I still could not handle myself in the manner that you and Maximus did when we were attacked by bandits."

"There's more to being a hero than just carrying a sword, although women quite like a man who can use a gladius. Of course they are also attracted to those men who wear a purse full of gold on their belt. I try to carry both, in order to narrow down the odds further," the optio said with a conspiratorial wink to the awkward looking youth. The bookish adolescent had trouble looking most people in the eye at the best of times.

"Unfortunately I'm as good with women as I am with a blade. I'm married too much to my studies," Arrian replied, forcing a half-smile. The diffident teenager was all theory and no practice when it came to the subject of women.

"Then you need to have an affair. I know an actress in Rome who is comfortable in playing with any part. Or I could always break Apollo's heart and arrange a tryst with his barmaid back at the tavern on the road home. I'm sensing that you're not that enamoured with German women. I hear that on the whole husbands stay faithful to their wives here. But they may well stay faithful because there's no one worth having an affair with. Yet tell me, has your sister ever been married? She is certainly old enough to have been married – and divorced – twice over by now," Atticus half-joked, nodding up ahead towards where Aurelia rode alongside Maximus.

Arrian had once heard her sister declare that she would not marry because she wanted to remain "a bride of Christ", but he resisted sharing this with the Roman soldier. He merely answered that Aurelia was still to marry – and then asked the optio if he had ever been wed, as he was old enough to have been divorced twice by now too.

"No, I've yet to embark upon that adventure, or suicide mission. It's also partly the reason why I've still gold in my purse, I warrant."

Arrian held out his palm and creased his face up in irritation as another shower broke out.

"You must not envy my homeland's weather."

"No, nor its fashions," Atticus quickly replied, creasing his face up in discomfort at having to wear Arrian's Germanic clothes. Aurelius needed to defeat the barbarians, if only for tunics to earn a victory over trousers for future generations, the soldier thought. "But all is context, as you may have realised in your studies. Germany is veritably arid compared to Britain, where I was once posted. I think the gods might cause it to rain so constantly there in order to help sober the natives up. Although sobering up a Briton may be a task too great for even a deity."

"And what are the women like over in Britain?" Arrian said, his curiosity overcoming his shyness.

"Somewhat closed-minded to Roman culture. But buy them a drink and they'll duly open up their hearts – and legs – to you," the soldier stated, smiling fondly as he recalled a pretty, bowlegged innkeeper's daughter from Londinium.

*

Maximus rode alongside Aurelia, but there were long periods where he did not utter a word to her, or indeed anyone. His strong jaw would clamp shut, as if a team of engineers would be needed to prize it open again. It was not the first time that Aurelia had witnessed the praetorian retreat into himself, inhabiting an internal forest far darker and more haunted than the one they were actually travelling through. Atticus had said how Maximus was never consciously being rude when he was taciturn. The optio told a story of how they had attended a dinner once in Rome. Maximus had sat towards the end of the table, silent, brooding. The wife of the host remarked how she had made a bet with her friend that the soldier would speak more than five words by the end of the meal. She hoped that she would win.

"You won't win your bet," Maximus laconically replied, remaining silent for the remainder of the dinner.

There had been instances of late, however, when the soldier had given himself over to talk to the German woman. Aurelia recalled how during the dinner the Emperor had hosted for them back at Aquileia she had subtly guided the conversation so Maximus spoke about his wife. At first he looked uncomfortable, even pained, talking about Julia but he forced himself to carry on. Aurelia began to realise just how much Maximus was devoted to her friend, how they drew strength from each other. "She was kind and she was beautiful – and in a way she taught me how being kind and being beautiful are one and the same thing," the soldier confessed, with a mixture of fondness and sorrow in his expression. She thought she saw tears begin to well in the usually gruff looking praetorian's eyes. He quickly excused himself, saying that he needed some air.

Aurelia wanted to now tell Maximus that she had known his wife, been her companion. Perhaps it would bring him some consolation and contentment when she spoke of the Julia she knew. Or maybe he would miss her more. She didn't want to deceive him anymore though. Did he know about Julia's faith and devotion to Christianity?

Aurelia drew breath, as if to give voice to her thoughts, but she was cut short by Maximus raising his hand. Up ahead were a group of armed men next to a white stone marker. They had reached the territory of her tribe. Half a dozen barbarians walked forward, carrying spears. She recognised the lead barbarian as Balloc, her father's illegitimate son. Whether Balloc recognised Aurelia or not the scowl across his face bespoke of his perpetual hostility towards anything and everyone. Even the news of him being pronounced his father's heir did not bring a smile to his sour features. A jagged, lightning bolt shaped scar ran down his cheek and scythed through his beard. Long, lank brown hair half covered the warrior's face. He barked a few words in his native language – and Arrian responded. The atmosphere was far from warm or familial as Balloc led the brother and sister away from the soldiers to talk in private. Before doing so Balloc ordered his men to keep a watchful eye on the Romans.

Maximus was impervious, indifferent, to the antagonistic looks and snorts of derision from the swarthy warriors as they pointed their spear tips towards him. His focus was on Aurelia. Should things turn nasty Maximus was ready to draw his sword, kick his heels into the flanks of his horse and protect her. He had grown to like and admire the headstrong woman over the past week. She appeared calm and authoritative when speaking with the more animated

Balloc. Her long black hair cascaded down her back. Her flattering figure even shone through the unflattering dress she was wearing. When Arrian had first spoken to Maximus during his recovery the German had praised his sister, describing her as intelligent, witty and kind. Finally the praetorian had reason to believe him.

"Do you think that we'll be welcomed with open arms when, or if, we reach the village? Or will they be up in arms?" Atticus remarked, eyeing the dour, hirsute figures around him with wariness and bemusement. Suddenly even the prospect of a dinner party with his father's friends seemed attractive, as opposed to the hospitality they might soon receive from the Arivisto.

17.

They reached the village within an hour or so. Balloc had ordered his men to walk either side of the Romans in order to guard, rather than protect, them. Occasionally he would turn and sneer at the soldiers – and Arrian – but otherwise he remained silent – making even Maximus appear garrulous.

There were a handful of stone cottages in the village but most dwellings were mud huts, or tents. Dozens of cooking pots bubbled away, filling the air with the smell of cabbage or onion soup. Occasionally a small, honey glazed boar turned upon a spit. The noise of a fast-flowing stream, as well as the bleating of livestock, could be heard in the background. The sound of laughter was conspicuous by its absence. When Atticus had set off from Aquileia he believed that he was dressed in little more than rags, but as he gazed around the village he felt veritably princely in his garb compared to the bedraggled natives. In some cases it seemed to be only the grime and mud that were still keeping the outfits together. Occasional flashes of colour could be seen though as some of the women – and men – wore braids, bangles and necklaces. Feral children played in the mud. Aside from the warrior class most people seemed malnourished and disease ridden. The smell of the onion soup couldn't quite overpower the ordure. The persistent drizzle raining down upon the village only added to the atmosphere of despondency and privation.

Maximus noted that there were plenty of well-armed men populating the settlement – and both the blacksmith and carpenter had queues forming around their places of business. Arrian had mentioned how the tribe were scattered throughout a number of villages. If other settlements possessed a similar quota of warriors then the

Arivisto could indeed prove to be a significant ally, or enemy. The strangers attracted a variety of looks, ranging from the mildly curious to the openly hostile. Sensing the attitude of their masters a trio of dogs even bared their teeth and growled at the visitors.

A young boy ran up to Balloc and handed him a large cup of wine, which he downed in one (albeit as much wine ran down his beard as ran down his throat). Balloc nodded his head and grunted, conveying to the child to tell Tarbus that the hunting party had returned.

As Arrian looked around him he was struck by how little the village had changed in his absence. The earthy odours filling his nostrils prompted memories; few of them were pleasant. Ironically some villagers walked by him and looked down their noses at the youth, as if he were a bad smell. He had never quite fitted in, even before he had ventured to Rome. He had failed as a hunter. He had failed in embracing the tribe's traditions and gods. And he had failed as a son. But somehow Arrian instinctively knew that there was something different, better, beyond the lands of the Arivisto – and Rome, or rather philosophy, had saved his soul.

Arrian gulped, his mouth went dry and he felt his being shrivel up like a raisin in the sun as he spotted his father coming towards him. Tarbus would have been an imposing figure even without the large battle-axe which he carried in his hand as a king might carry a sceptre. He was a man used to being feared and revered (indeed the two were one and the same in his mind). Arrian had not inherited his father's tall, broad build. Indeed the student sometimes wondered if he had inherited anything from his father, to the point of believing that he may not even be his son. Bushy eyebrows hung over a pair of cunning, cruel eyes (as opposed to Balloc's aspect, which seemed solely concerned with cruelty). The other villagers gave their chieftain a wide birth as he strode forward, mud splashing up from his heavy gait.

A sense of menace and brutality oozed out of him, like sweat. Maximus could barely work out where the chief's scraggly beard ended and equally where his scraggly fur coat began (should Galen have been present he could have informed the soldier that the belt fastened around the great coat was partly made of human bones). The barbarian's beard concealed a bull-neck and increasingly jowly face. Maximus briefly glanced at the huge axe, stained with blood and rust that Tarbus carried in his large, scarred right hand. The praetorian nodded his head in respect as the chief stood before him.

Tarbus grunted and knitted his brow at seeing his estranged son, but his craggy features softened as he took in his daughter. She smiled and bowed – and his demeanour softened even more. Father and daughter exchanged a few words and he clasped her hands in his. The re-union began to attract the attention of the whole village. To some, fuelled by the propaganda of Balloc, "Arrian" was a dirty word, or an insult. He had turned his back on the tribe and sold his soul to the enemy. He had even taken a Roman name, to add injury to the insult.

Tarbus looked on with stony indifference or boredom even as his son spoke. Arrian first remarked how glad he was to see his father and to have returned home – and then he reported on how he had been asked by the Emperor to discuss the prospect of an alliance between Rome and the Arivisto. The tribe could no longer afford to remain neutral in the war. Rome was willing to offer generous trade subsidies to the tribe, as well as arm and supply its warriors. At this point, conscious of all the suspicious faces glaring at him, Arrian asked his father if he wanted to retreat somewhere to discuss the terms of the alliance in private.

"I have no desire to discuss anything in private with you. I have no secrets from my tribe, as a father has no secrets from his children. It is strange that a son should keep things from his father though. Do you think that we should be

77

bowing before you and hailing your name for negotiating with the Romans on our behalf? You probably think you have been clever, no? Perhaps you were inspired by someone in a story in one of your precious books," Tarbus remarked, spitting out a gob of phlegm as he did so, as if the act represented what he thought of his son and his books.

Balloc sniggered, which in turn encouraged others around him to do so.

"Please, father, do not dismiss what he has to say. I believe the Emperor to be a good man," Aurelia said, stepping forward to do so. She cut short her speech however at seeing her father raise his hand, giving her a fierce look as he did so.

"I'm pleased to see you again, daughter. But women should be seen and not heard. Now hear this, both of you. You do not bet on the fighter who has been knocked down. You do not try to save an injured animal. You kill it – put it out of its misery. Rome has been wounded, bloodied. It will not and cannot win a significant battle against the Marcomanni and its allies. Your Caesar may be a good man, but he is not a good commander. You were a stupid, deluded boy when you left for Rome. You have returned a stupid, deluded man. But you were right in one regard. The Arivisto cannot remain neutral any longer. Everyone must choose a side. I have negotiated an alliance with Balomar – a strong commander rather than a good, weak man."

Aurelia's eyes widened in shock and peril and she immediately turned to Maximus. Her face conveyed an apology and also a plea for help. Although the soldier was unable to understand a word of the exchange between father and son he could intuit that all was not well. His suspicions were confirmed when, head downcast, Arrian remarked, "My father has made an alliance with Balomar."

Tarbus nodded at Balloc, at which point the young warrior growled out an order. Spear tips were raised.

Maximus and Atticus struggled not as they were restrained and disarmed.

Aurelia's mouth was agape and a look of pity could now been seen on her pale face, as she gazed at the centurion. Her heart went out to him.

"I'm sorry," Arrian said, ashamed and saddened. Had the praetorian saved his life, twice, and journeyed halfway across the continent for things to come to this?

"Don't worry, it won't be you who'll be sorry," Maximus replied – speaking to Arrian but staring at Tarbus. Unflinching. Undefeated.

18.

"Looks like we're in the shit again," Rufus Atticus remarked, arching his eyebrow and looking down at the floor of the cage, which was littered with animal excrement. The soldiers had been placed in a cage, which the tribe usually used to store wild boars or livestock.

Darkness had fallen. A couple of torches, either side of the cage, still illuminated the scene. At least the villagers had now turned in for the night. They'd thankfully grown tired of firing off curses – and stones and mud – at the prisoners.

"Do you think they'll ransom us?" Atticus added. "If so then I fear my father may pay the tribe to keep me, rather than set me free. What do you make of our odds in getting out of this?"

"A one wheeled chariot has more chance of winning a race in the Circus Maximus," the centurion posited.

"So we've been in worse situations then?"

"Aye," Maximus replied, staring off into the distance. The praetorian was only half concentrating on his grim-humoured exchange with his optio. His thoughts had turned to Marcus Aurelius. The soldier had given his word to the Emperor that he would return before the army crossed the Danube at Pannonia. Not only had Maximus never broken his word to his Emperor before, but he worried for the army should Aurelius be given poor counsel. He did not want augurs and religious leaders getting their claws into his commander. Nero may have made his horse a member of the Senate, but not even he would have given control of his legions over to a priest.

"The omens are good," Salvidius, an oleaginous augur with a penchant for collecting fine pottery and young slave boys, had portentously remarked to the Emperor during a recent war council.

"More importantly, the troops are ready," Maximus stated, his manner as hard as iron.

"You will soon win a great victory Emperor and after the battle we will praise and honour the gods," Salvidius later said, stroking his grey beard with his heavily ringed fingers.

"The first thing we will do, after winning any battle, will be to praise and honour the wounded and dead," Maximus countered. "Soldiers win battle, unless your gods want to don some armour and stand in a shield wall like the rest of us."

*

The night air chilled his sweat-soaked skin. Arrian trod as stealthily as he could over the glutinous ground. With every step he felt like he was sinking deeper into the mud – and deeper into trouble. Few who defied Tarbus of the Arivisto lived. He'd had little appetite over dinner – and not just because the food was about as palatable as his father's politics. Tarbus had sat Aurelia next to him – and also close to an ogling Balloc. Arrian however had been ordered to sit at the opposite end of the table, next to a couple of burly warriors who stank as much as the cage the Romans had been imprisoned in. The only time his father acknowledged him was when he ridiculed him. The rest of the table would then laugh, akin to the Chorus in a Greek tragedy. There had only been a brief moment during the evening when Arrian could speak freely with his sister.

"We need to save them. Tonight," he had whispered.

"Agreed," she replied.

Arrian saw his sister's silhouette melt into the night as she went to ready the horses. The cage was in sight. Thankfully the guard watching the prisoners appeared to be asleep. The key to the large iron lock, which fastened the doors to the cage, sat away from the guard on a stool. The sentry would have to be silenced though.

Maximus gave a nod of thanks and encouragement to the young German as he approached. Arrian's hand trembled slightly, both with fear and from the cold, as he handed the knife to the praetorian through the bars of the cage. The student averted his eyes, not wishing to see what would follow. The centurion would cup his hand over the guard's mouth and cut his way through his windpipe and neck. But Maximus was stopped in his tracks, by the sound of booming laughter and slow clapping.

"Ha, finally you're of some use boy and I'm grateful for you being alive. I had a bet with Balloc. He wagered that you would not help your friends because you'd be cowardly. I said that you would, because you were too stupid," Tarbus announced in a rough, contemptuous voice. Dozens of torches lit up, like giant fireflies, in the darkness. Shaggy, fur-clad figures came out from behind tents. The Arivisto formed a horseshoe around the prisoner – and traitor. Arrian pressed his back against the bars of the cage. Dread cut itself into his features. Atticus placed a consoling hand upon his shoulder.

"You did your best. We're grateful. And never mind your father, you proved me right. You don't have to carry a sword to be a hero."

Everyone's attention now turned to the sight of Balloc, dragging Aurelia by the arm. He grunted as he pushed the woman into the mud, in front of her brother. Arrian helped his sister up and they hugged. Tears began to stream down both of their cheeks. Fury and a sense of futility vied for the sovereignty of Maximus' being.

"Come here boy. You always were a cry baby. I remember you as a child, you used to water the crops more than the rain... Come here, I won't hurt you."

As if he were a child again Arrian obeyed. He hung his head and dutifully approached his father. All seemed lost. He would never be able to return to Rome, see his tutors or read his books again. He would never be able to attend the theatre, or baths. He would be condemned to live as an outcast within the tribe. A slave. Or his father would put him in a shield wall and sentence him to death. Yet death seemed a welcome fate, compared to the living death which was the alternative.

Tarbus viciously slapped his son across the face with the back of his hand, giving vent to his animus. The rings on his fingers sliced through Arrian's cheek and nose. The student fell to the ground. Blood rather than tears ran down his face. Aurelia let out a plea, to both God and her father, to spare her brother. She could barely be heard above the cheers and curses of the tribe however. Wine dulled their sense of compassion – and fuelled their ire.

"You've dedicated your miserable life to studying boy. Well I'm about to teach you your final lesson – show you what happens when you betray your own people," Tarbus proclaimed, as much for his tribe's benefit as for his son's ears.

The chieftain gave a solemn nod of his head. Even before Maximus heard the sound of Balloc's sword scrape out of its scabbard he knew Arrian's fate. There was a look of satisfaction, even glee, on his face as Balloc strode up to his half-brother and shoved the point of his sword into his victim's neck. Before, or as he did so however, Arrian remembered a quote from Epicurus:

Death does not concern us, because as long as we exist, death is not here. And when it does come, we no longer exist.

This time everyone heard Aurelia scream. She rushed to her brother. Blood gurgled out from the glistening wound. There was a look of shock, rather than the usual sweet expression, on Arrian's ashen face.

"You should not mourn a traitor, daughter. I hope that Rome has not turned your head – and poisoned your heart – as well. You can finally come back home. Your future is with the Arivisto," Tarbus announced. He had promised his daughter to Balloc, to secure the bloodline within the tribe, but he might also be able to strengthen his alliance with the Marcomanni by giving his daughter to Balomar.

Balloc turned to the cheering crowd, raising his arms and gore-stained blade as if he were a gladiator who had just won a great victory in the arena. The warrior bared his teeth and stuck his tongue out when he turned to Atticus – but the optio altered not his own expression. He merely gazed upon the bastard son of Tarbus as if he were already a corpse.

Aurelia rose to her feet and stared at her father as though he was already dead to her. It was not that she thought that he had changed during her time in Rome, but rather it was she who looked at him with new eyes. Aurelia felt she had nothing more to say to the chief of the Arivisto. She was too sad, shocked and angry.

Rain commenced to slap upon the muddy ground. The stars seemed to dim in mourning. The sister bent down, closed her brother's eyes and lovingly kissed him on the forehead. She squeezed his hand, as she used to do to bring him comfort and confidence when he was alive. The woman then wordlessly walked towards the cage. She retrieved the key from the stool, unlocked the door and entered. Aurelia felt safer and freer imprisoned with the Romans – more so than if she were queen of all the German tribes. She would share the fate of the captives and her brother. The crowd watched in part disbelief, part curiosity. Aurelia fell into the centurion's arms and buried her face into his chest.

Tarbus' disappointment in his daughter quickly turned to disdain. "So be it," he said with a snort. "But I expected better from you."

Aurelia heard her father's words and was tempted to reply that she expected better from him too, but she remained silent. She just clung to the praetorian – for if she let go of him Aurelia felt she might fall.

"If they decide to execute us tomorrow I'm taking a few of the bastards, or one bastard in particular, with me to meet the ferryman," Atticus remarked, still staring at a triumphant Balloc.

Maximus nodded in reply. If Tarbus came within an arm's reach he would break his neck.

"You can all stew in there until the morning. It could be the last dawn you see. As for the rest of you the show is over. Go back to your beds. Get some rest. For tomorrow we set off to join our German brothers – and we will wash our spears in the blood of the Roman imperialist scum," the chief shouted, over the increasing roar of the rain.

"I'm sorry," Aurelia murmured, looking up at Maximus – apologising for everything, for things that the soldier was unaware of. "We're damned."

"No. We can still be saved. Have faith," the praetorian whispered back, determined that his war wouldn't be over so soon.

19.

Atticus eventually drifted off to sleep, with thoughts of how he would get close to Balloc on his mind. He had sharpened a flat stone and would slice it across his enemy's neck. They would kill him for the crime – but they couldn't execute him twice, so it was a worthwhile venture, the optio reasoned. He was dead anyway. Tarbus would not ransom them now. Atticus wished that he could write to Claudia, or to give instructions to a friend in regards to publishing his poetry. But, as he confided to his centurion, "I don't have any regrets – aside from being captured and sentenced to die of course."

It was deep into the night. Even the owls and nightingales had gone to sleep. The sentry also slept, this time in earnest, occasionally snoring.

Maximus and Aurelia were still awake, however, sitting next to each other. The praetorian had given the woman his cloak to wrap around her. Yet her convulsions were from sobbing, rather than shivering from the cold. Aurelia turned her head to glance at the soldier. As usual his stony expression was unreadable. She knew not how he would react when she offered up her confession. But she was compelled to finally do so. Her voice, like her heart, cracked occasionally as she spoke. She stared straight ahead of her, fearful of breaking down should she look the widower in the eye.

"I need to tell you something. You might be tempted to interrupt, but please let me finish. I need to tell you things, while I still can. I knew Julia, she was my friend. We got to know each other while you were on campaign in Parthia. I loved her like a sister – an older, wiser sister. She made me laugh. She taught me the meaning of friendship."

Aurelia heard Maximus take a deep breath, as if he were about to speak, but she placed her hand upon his and carried on speaking, before he could interject.

"Julia became a Christian. I may have introduced her to my religion, but she gave herself to God freely. I think that God was in her life before she even met me. He had called out to her. Christianity just gave her a name to call back to... But you were important to her as well. She once told me that she loved you before she even met you. She loved the idea of you... I once believed that Julia had to choose between you and God. In some ways I was jealous of you, the hold you had over her. I was wrong to think such things. She argued that, in knowing you, she found love. And, in knowing love, she found God... We drifted apart, just before you returned to Rome. I never got to say goodbye or to apologise to her... When I met you I hated you, because you reminded me of her. I was also prejudiced against soldiers. The army captured and executed many of my friends. Not all Christians may be Christian, but most are. They were good people – and I wrongly held you responsible for their deaths. But yet I'm glad you're here with me now, partly because you remind me of Julia. You carry a part of her in you."

Aurelia felt Maximus squeeze her hand. His whole body seemed to tense up. The icy wind blew through the bars of the cage, sighing.

"Julia's still part of me – the best part of me. But there is also a hole in my life, where she once lived. I try to fill the emptiness with grief, work, drink and anger. Yet when it comes to the last thing at night, or the first thing in the morning, the emptiness is still there. It's like a wound – and the stitches keep bursting... Julia told me about her religion. She would often even read the Gospels and other texts to me. She also mentioned a friend that she wanted me to meet, who introduced her to your congregation. You made her laugh too... But Julia worried about you increasingly though, when she wrote to me. She thought that you were devoting yourself too much to religion, as opposed to God…Her faith brought to her a sense of comfort and contentment. In the end, she said that God was calling to her. I urged her to ignore his call though and stay with me. Heaven has enough angels, by all accounts. This world has fewer. If you were jealous of Julia's love for me, I grew jealous of her devotion to God... She said that she was at peace, when the end finally came. I'm still not at peace though. If your God exists, then he took my wife and children from me. If he wants me to give him service, over and above that which I owe to Caesar, then pray to him to give them back."

The soldier's tone was imbued with as much grief as it was resentment. He sighed again, as if Maximus wanted to expel all the life, as well as air, out of him too.

"I believe you to be a good man, Maximus. And in being good, you are already giving service to God."

"Julia often said that God works in mysterious ways. Just to see her again in the next life will be reward enough for any scrap of good I can do on earth."

"When the congregation disbanded and then Julia passed away there was a part of me that wanted to die too. I feel like that again. I've got nothing, no one, to live for," Aurelia mournfully issued, her hand now limp in his.

Maximus wanted to say that she had him. Aurelia wanted him to say it too. The lambent moon came out from behind the clouds and lit up their faces as they turned to each other. Maximus smiled and squeezed her hand – and she responded in kind. They shared a moment.

Their moment was cut short however by the sight of Apollo slitting the throat of the snoring sentry.

20.

Atticus rubbed the sleep – and disbelief – out of his eyes at seeing the young legionary open the door to their prison, wiping the bloody blade that his centurion had given him on his trousers.

"Hope for the best, plan for the worst," Maximus expressed by way of an explanation. The praetorian had instructed Apollo to track his party from the moment they left Aquileia. For the past few hours the archer had posted himself in a large oak tree, overlooking the village and his centurion, biding his time.

"You could've told me."

"I thought you liked surprises."

"I must confess, I'm enjoying this one," the optio said, his semblance filled with gratitude and respect for the new recruit. Apollo's boyish grin widened even more in reply. They moved with stealth and speed into the forest. It would be dawn soon however and their absence would quickly be discovered. There was a danger that Tarbus could use his hunting dogs to track the fugitives. Aurelia in particular would need a head start if she was to make it back across the Danube. Yet Maximus had already formed a plan to keep the Arivisto occupied.

"Did you bring the fire arrows?"

"Aye, it wouldn't very well be a party without them," Apollo answered, exhilarated rather than scared by the situation they were all in. Drills, marching and sentry duty were not half as much fun, or as meaningful, as the mission as he was on now.

"Atticus, I need you to take Aurelia and head back towards the nearest fort on the other side of the Danube. Get a message to the Emperor, brief him on the Arivisto's alliance with Balomar. I won't be too far behind."

"No, we won't leave you. We should stay together," Aurelia anxiously argued, not wishing the praetorian to sacrifice himself, or be parted from her.

"Neither you, nor your father, can get rid of me that easily, don't worry. I promise I'll be following close behind you both. Apollo and I just need to give the village a wake-up call."

"I can help the lad out if needs be," Atticus volunteered, not wanting his friend to potentially sacrifice himself either. He sensed that he was Aurelia's second choice in escorting her back to the fort.

"With your aim with a bow you'll more likely set fire to Pompeii from here. No, both of you, go now," Maximus said, with a blend of warmth and sternness. His gazed rested on the beautiful, Christian woman for a couple of extra, telling seconds – and the eerie atmosphere of the forest was fleetingly coloured by an air of romance. He hoped that he would see her once more. As much as they had recently shared, it felt like their story had only half been told.

Aurelia embraced the young legionary and thanked him for saving them all, with a kiss. Even in the dim light of the forest Atticus noticed Apollo crimson. He'd been kissed before – but never by a lady. The optio bid the recruit a fond farewell also.

"You're a god send Apollo. When we next visit a tavern back in Rome I'll make sure you won't be able to stand the following morning, from the drink and women that I'll treat you to… Keep saving the life of your centurion too. You never know, he might just put you on latrine duty only every other night as a thank you."

Aurelia embraced Maximus. She held onto him for a couple of extra, telling seconds, and whispered something in his ear.

*

The dawn light glowed in the distance, but the village burned brighter. Apollo had reported with relish how the

Arivisto stored their hay and heating oil together in the barn. Each flaming arrow struck its intended target as the two accomplished archers rained havoc down upon their enemy. The air spat and crackled with fire. Plumes of smoke billowed up into the sky. For once the Arivisto would have welcomed the sight of grey clouds and rain. Flames devoured tents and wattle and daub houses in minutes. Villagers scattered themselves like ants, torn between saving their possessions and combating the blaze. The fate of the village duly eclipsed the fate of the escaped prisoners. Tarbus was as enflamed as his surroundings though when he discovered the empty cage and the murdered sentry. He vowed to join his allies as soon as possible and take the fight to Rome. "There will be blood," he snarled.

As tempted as Maximus was to watch the settlement burn – and get Tarbus in his sights – he headed for home as soon as their fire arrows were all spent. The praetorian would keep his promise to his Emperor and join him when he crossed the Danube. The legions had little need to advance northwards however – for Balomar had marched south.

21.

A light drizzle hazed up the air and diluted the afternoon sun. The great turquoise river flowed on, blissfully ignorant of the dreams, actions and follies of the people scurrying about all along its banks. As a philosopher Marcus Aurelius gazed at the undulating water and was reminded of a meditation that he had recently composed: *Time is a river of passing events and its current is strong; no sooner is a thing brought to sight than it is swept by and another takes its place, and this too will be swept away.* Time, Life and Nature were all so much greater than the war with the Marcomanni, than Rome itself.

As a Caesar, however, he stared at the river and starkly thought to himself, *the Danube is my Rubicon.*

The Emperor sat astride his dapple grey horse and pensively looked out across at the opposing shore. The birch and willow trees looked the same on the other side, the bird song sounded the same and the sunlight would be no brighter or dimmer across the Danube – but everything would change when he reached the other side. History's pen hung over him, like the Sword of Damocles. Would he be the Emperor who saved, or damned, the Empire? The stoic in him bore the burden without complaint, but Marcus Aurelius the man felt frail, anxious, lonely – human. As Emperor he could have chosen to remain in Rome. He could have delegated his command to another. He could have been having lunch with his wife, Faustina, in the imperial palace right now, he mused. He would have been nodding incessantly, listening to her gossip and news about what she bought whilst out shopping during the morning (whilst in his head Aurelius would have attended to the business of the state). Or he could have been reading to his son right now and teaching him Euclid. Both of their faces would have lit up too as the wisdom of Socrates and poetry of Horace took root in his fledgling intellect and soul. But duty called. Would it be his Siren song?

Aurelius sat with his back to his advisers and army, concealing the anguish and indecision which lined his ageing face. The Emperor's cloak hung around him, disguising how he was doubled-over in discomfort (or rather pain) from a returning stomach complaint. Galen could help relieve some of the symptoms, but he could not remedy a cure. He suffered in silence.

His expression had remained as unmoved as one of his statues when a messenger had delivered the news that the Arivisto had formed an alliance with the Marcomanni. The Emperor could not help but emit a sigh of relief at hearing that Maximus had returned safely though. The sigh of relief turned to one of grief soon after however when he heard the news that Arrian had been murdered. He had liked the student. He had not held the blade, but was he not guilty of killing him?

Aurelius rode at the vanguard of his army. He was but accompanied by a few cohorts at present, as the rest of the army negotiated the marshes and forests of the province of Pannonia. His scouts had just reported that the enemy were making their way back north, from having executed a number of raids in Roman territory. The Marcomanni were in striking distance. The army were awaiting Caesar's orders.

His officers had advised caution. They should wait for the rest of the legions to form up, before engaging the enemy. By the time that would happen however there wouldn't be an enemy to engage. It remained unspoken how the legions had still to best the enemy in combat when the numbers had been equal – and from the scout's report the force of barbarians was even greater than that of their cohorts.

What would Maximus do? The Emperor knew the answer to the question he posed to himself, before even asking it.

Maximus would take the fight to the enemy and believe in the courage and skill of the legions. He would argue that his officers were advising caution because they were more concerned with not losing a battle, as opposed to winning one.

Whether it was due to the cold air, or due to the fact that he had never drawn it before and the blade needed oiling, Aurelius struggled slightly to unsheathe his sword. But unsheathe it he did. The weapon felt heavy and alien in his hands – but he could and would get used to the sensation.

The die is cast.

The Emperor turned to face his council of war. Despite the pain he sat up straight on his horse. He instructed his senior centurions to form up the cohorts. They were marching eastwards. They were going to engage the enemy. He quickly dispatched messengers to order the legions to turn eastwards too.

"But, Caesar, should we not consult the auspices as to the merit of engaging the enemy? Surely the Emperor would want to know if he has the gods on his side?" Salvidius anxiously exclaimed, having no wish to be by his commander's side when he gave battle.

"Who needs the gods when you've got the Praetorian Guard," Maximus expressed, as he trotted up to the senior staff, alongside Atticus.

Apollo shrugged his shoulders, though he could have answered more honestly if he just nodded his head and declared that he was nervous. Indeed he was scared. The elation and encouragement from succeeding in his previous mission had subsided.

"Do you remember your first battle Atticus?"

"Well it's not the sort of thing you want to relive regularly. But I can recall some of it. Self-preservation, more than courage, compelled me to fight on. Just when you think that you can't hold up your shield any longer you discover that you can, as an axe may come down and cut you in two if you don't still hold it aloft. And just when you think that your arm is about to fall off from thrusting your sword forward again and again you'll find the will and strength to do so – again and again – else the enemy will stab your friend standing next to you in the shield wall. I remember my thoughts before the engagement too. I wanted to prove my father wrong, who believed that I wasn't cut out for the army. I ran through my drills and training in my head. I also pictured which one of my past girlfriends would look best in black at my funeral. But you're going to be fine Apollo. It's just unfortunate that Aurelia is still back at the fort. You won't receive another kiss once it's all over."

A smile broke the tension in the legionary's face, amused and embarrassed as he was in equal measure. Apollo did not want to let Atticus and Maximus down. They believed that he was not just cut out for the army – they considered him good enough for the Praetorian Guard. He did not want to earn a promotion and then not live to see his first pay packet.

"Don't worry lad. When we get back to Rome I'll introduce you to some women who'll do more than just kiss a war hero. Their husbands are far more interested in politics, or boys even younger than you. Or both. When you tell them that you were at the battle of Pannonia they'll devour you like a lioness would a lamb."

"That'd be one fight that I'd be happy to lose," the bright-eyed archer replied, his hands no longer shaking.

23.

The clouds parted to reveal a crisp blue sky, as if the Gods wanted a better view of the imminent contest. Three ranks of legionaries were lined across the plain, between the tree line and river bank. A mass of barbarians were similarly forming up – preparing to swarm. Some donned headbands to keep the hair out their eyes. Some smeared their faces with blue or red dye. Some jeered, or howled in intimidation and exhilaration. Most were seasoned warriors, buoyed by a number of successful raids in enemy territory. At the head of the formidable force stood Tangan, Balomar's brutal second in command. Tangan had a taste for raping women, in the sight of their husbands. He possessed the bulk of a wrestler, but the speed of a Thracian gladiator. His beard and long greasy hair billowed in the breeze as he repeatedly thrust his spear in the air, with its giant leaf-shaped blade, in time to spitting out a guttural war cry.

Maximus stood in the centre of the front rank of legionaries. He eyed the opposing force believing that discipline could overcome ferocity – method could triumph over madness.

"They bark and howl like dogs. So let us put them down like dogs… Remember how much Roman blood they have spilled. Let us now soak their lands in their blood… The Emperor has put his faith in us, so let us repay the compliment… Pannonia will be carved into the annals of our history. Immortal fame beckons. We are adding a verse into the song of swords. But you will not just be rewarded with a sense of pride and eternal fame… German food may be bland. German wine may be acidic. And according to Atticus their women taste sour. But victory against the Marcomanni will taste sweet. We will relieve them of their plunder and be rewarded in this life, as well as the next… Do not break formation. Let them come to us, throw themselves on our spears and swords…"

Maximus, after bolstering his men's courage, offered up a silent prayer, to Julia's God as well as Jupiter, that Rome, the Emperor, would be victorious – even if he had to sacrifice himself. He remembered Arrian. A part of the widower had envied his young friend. He had found peace.

*

Balomar, his expression as hard as flint, watched on from across the Danube. His body was taut with muscle – and expectation. Tangan, standing before his warriors, would serve as the tip to the blade which would scythe through the Roman lines. The great king of the Marcomanni wore short leather trousers and a studded leather jerkin. Small scars marked his bald head, from where it had crashed down upon various noses, check bones and jaws over the years. He wore a large gold torc around his neck, a prize stolen from a Dacian tribal chief who had dared to challenge him to a duel. He gazed intently, his aspect filled with either fire or ice, at his army forming up, preparing to advance. He smiled in satisfaction, revealing a pair of fangs for front teeth from where he had once chipped them in a fight – and filed them into shape afterwards. As a result the king often hissed as he spoke. Some of his warriors would, quite literally, eat the hearts of their vanquished foes. The ground would soon be awash with Roman blood, of the dead rather than just wounded too. Mercy was an indulgence – exercised by either the all-powerful or the weak. Was that the Emperor himself taking to the field too? Aurelius had experienced Balomar's guile – now he would suffer his martial prowess. Should he capture Aurelius – he would then kill him. Like Achilles with Hector he would drag his body after his chariot and send his corpse back to Rome, looking all too mortal. After today no one would have to live under the yoke of Rome. Balomar would show his enemies that the Germanic people were the master race.

*

Beer and wine fired their spirits, but they would also dull their wits and coordination Maximus thought to himself. The enemy advanced in the shape of an arrowhead, or wedge. Crows flew in and perched upon the trees, cawing in expectation of the feast to follow. The Marcomanni possessed few horsemen. Balomar would save his cavalry for when the Romans routed – and they could cut down the fleeing legionaries. A few of the troops started to shuffle nervously in the shield wall, but Maximus, Atticus and other veterans moved forward slightly, rather than back.

In an act of bravery, or lunacy, Tangan broke off from his army and ran forward as if to take on the enemy alone. Blood lust, or wine, spurred him on. He raised his shield (a Roman one, a spoil of war from a previous engagement). Perhaps his intention was to provoke the legionaries into firing their javelins at him. Still he ran forward, kicking up mud like a horse. The Marcomanni cheered their champion on. Maximus thought that he would give his own troops something to cheer about though. He broke ranks from the shield wall and drew his gladius, running towards the hulking warrior. They closed upon each other in the open space between the two armies. Maximus feinted to the right and Tangan stabbed his spear forward with a roar. The praetorian quickly darted to the left however, as the leaf-shaped blade of his enemy sliced through thin air; Maximus span and buried his blade into the side of Tangan's head. The warrior fell to the ground immediately. Some paused in the ranks of the Marcomanni, aghast that their champion could be cut down so quickly. Others were enraged though, as if oil had just been poured onto a fire. They charged, earlier than the aghast and furious Balomar, observing the engagement from across the river, would have liked.

Maximus took his place again in the centre of the shield wall. Men cheered and patted him on the back.

"If you live through this you might get a medal," Atticus said, tightening the chin strap on his helmet.

"The only thing I'll want to get, if we live through this, is drunk," the centurion replied, in earnest.

The line of Roman soldiers was slightly curved, so that the two wings had a better angle to fire their javelins from. The volley of spears from the rear rank skewered into flesh and shields; but still they came. The battle-cries grew in volume and ferocity. Many a legionary uttered a prayer beneath his breath, or pictured a loved one – before his thoughts turned to the business of killing. Some of the more experienced soldiers bucked backwards before transferring their weight forwards – thrusting their bodies and large scutums into the oncoming enemy. The human wave crashed into the human dam. It bent, but did not break. Yelling, howling, screaming, the crunch of shields against shields and the ring of blades upon blades erupted into the air, over and over again – separately, yet one continuous sound.

Blood soon flecked the faces of Romans and barbarians alike. The churned up muddy ground reddened. Legionaries stood behind their shields, relentlessly stabbing their swords out into shins and faces – tapping into the muscle memory of hundreds of drills. A few of the legionaries fell but the gap was immediately filled by the reserve ranks.

Some of the Marcomanni possessed mail or plate armour, but most didn't. The Romans were well-equipped, well-provisioned, well-trained. Although the Emperor had yet to win a major battle he had quickly mastered the art of logistics, in regards to his army. No detail escaped his judicious eye. The army was more loyal to Marcus Aurelius than many in the Senate thought. Rations found themselves into the bellies of soldiers, rather than onto wagons belonging to bureaucrats or quartermasters. Discipline was maintained not just through a culture of corporal punishments.

Balomar watched on, his nostrils flared in rage. Although he could not quite make out which side was gaining the momentum the Roman line had yet to break. But the sheer weight of numbers would surely tell, like a pack of hyenas bringing down a lion.

24.

Some of the barbarians called it "the Whisper of Death" – the sound of a Roman arrow swishing through the air. But the whisper grew louder as dozens of archers appeared from out of the tree line and fired missile after missile into the tightly packed ranks of the enemy. Apollo didn't even check to see whether his arrows hit the mark. Instead he just concentrated on firing off the next one. Every shaft which struck an enemy meant that there was one less barbarian capable of killing his friends.

"Keep firing lad. Don't stop till you meet a Gaul who doesn't surrender, a Greek who pays his debts or a Briton who's sober," a rough-voiced, grizzled comrade exclaimed.

The remaining cohort also appeared from out of the woods and launched their javelins, arcing them over the first line of barbarians (who had turned and raised their shields towards the new enemy) into the centre of the opposing force. Confusion and fear, as much as death, swept through the Marcomanni. Some of the enemy started to move backwards, whilst others still surged forward, looking to engage the Roman lines. Curse-spitting warriors commenced to trip over the living and the dead. The left side of Balomar's army started to buckle and thin out. The Roman cohort formed up from out of the trees and advanced. The flanking manoeuvre not only gave the main contingent of the Emperor's army time to pause and re-strengthen its ranks, but such was the loss of the Marcomanni's momentum that Maximus ordered a slow advance. The injured foes who they stepped over were methodically stabbed in the neck or groin.

*

Galen had recently tried to give encouragement to the Emperor by arguing, through a syllogism, that warfare was merely problem solving. Aurelius was adept at problem solving. Therefore he was adept at warfare. Aurelius sat upon his horse on the high ground behind his army and thought how warfare was more akin to conducting a group of musicians. He hoped that he had timed the introduction of his archers and reserve cohort well. He had marvelled at the way his soldiers had stood there during the initial onslaught – and he thought of Maximus, leading and representing the legionaries. *Be like a headland of rock on which the waves crash upon incessantly. But the rock stands fast and the seething waters eventually settle.* Hope began to triumph over worry as Aurelius saw his troops drive the enemy backwards – and also closer to the river.

*

Balomar cursed the Roman army – and then his own – as he saw sections of his forces begin to retreat. Many of them had little desire to fall during the final battle of their campaigning season. Dead men can't enjoy their spoils of war. Balomar realised that much of his own plunder was still loaded on wagons, on the wrong side of the bridge. One wagon in particular carried enough gold to finance his regiments of mercenaries for the coming year. He called for Tarbus. It was time to blood his new allies in battle.

*

Some shed their furs and dived into the Danube with the intention being to swim to the opposite bank. Some disappeared into the forest. Some ran back to the bridge and baggage train, looking to secure their valuables (as well as the valuables of their comrades). Some fought on, because they had to – or because they believed that they could still defeat the enemy.

Maximus continued to bellow out orders for the men around him to keep their shape. At the same time he also sent an order to his fellow centurions on his right to wheel the line around and envelop the left side of the enemy army.

The wave that had once crashed about their shore was now a tide that was retreating.

Defeat for the Marcomanni turned into a rout when Maximus felt the ground shudder at the arrival of a cavalry detachment. After hearing about the possible spoils of war to be won a decurion had requested permission from his commanding officer to race ahead of the legion and join the Emperor. The legate acceded to the request (on condition he receive a cut of any possible plunder). The cheers – and sighs of relief – could just about be heard over the rolling thunder of their galloping hooves as horsemen streamed out onto the battlefield. They swarmed – and stung.

*

No one perhaps sighed in relief, or inwardly cheered, as much as Marcus Aurelius himself. Sweat soaked his reins from having gripped them so tightly.

"The gods have granted us victory," Salvidius remarked to the Emperor, shortly after sighing with relief also.

"Mortals have granted us victory today. Deities had nothing to do with it. Unfortunately too many have proved just how mortal they were," the Emperor mournfully replied. He hoped that Gaius Maximus was still alive. Not even the Emperor of Rome had the power within him to resurrect and thank a dead man.

*

Maximus finally had a chance to catch his breath and survey the battlefield. His arm, up to his elbow, was crimson (soldiering was sometimes little more than butchery, he sometimes thought). The Danube, which for so long had served as a protective moat for the northern tribes, was now a cause of their end as many fleeing warriors lost their fight with the strong currents and drowned. He saw Apollo, close to him, pull arrows out of corpses and re-fire them at the enemy. The praetorian glanced behind him to see if the Emperor was still on the ridge but it appeared that he had, along with his bodyguards and the senior staff, repositioned himself. Maximus just hoped that Aurelius hadn't retreated just before he could have witnessed his hour of triumph. Partly due to the lure of the baggage train – and partly perhaps that they could have been isolated and counter-attacked if they crossed over the river alone, the cavalry concentrated on scything down the enemy on the southern side of the Danube. As such, realising that safety resided on the other side of the river, a tide of people surged across the bridge. Yet Maximus could not help but recognise a familiar figure swimming against the stream.

"Atticus, Apollo. Collect up as many arrows and archers to hand. We're going hunting."

25.

Tarbus looked like he had swallowed a wasp, which had been coated in vinegar, after Balomar ordered him to retrieve the strong box on the Roman side of the bridge. Partly the chief of the Arivisto was more used to giving than following commands. He took consolation from the fact however that at least his tribesmen had not been ordered to take part in the main offensive against the enemy. Yet Tarbus felt now an itch, as potent as the pox, that he had formed an alliance with the wrong side in the war.

Balloc and half a dozen other warriors joined their leader as they attempted to cross the bridge in the opposite direction to everyone else. Tarbus brandished his fearsome weapon, in hope that the waves of people ahead of him would be inclined to move asunder. He shoved and barked at the throng, his ire still burning from the fire in his settlement. The damage to the village would take months to fully repair. Tarbus yearned to swing his battle-axe at anything – and no matter who he slaughtered he would picture his enemy as the stone-faced praetorian.

Yet the vengeful chieftain stared across the battlefield to witness Maximus already moving towards him, though there was a line of Marcomanni warriors between them.

*

A giant horseshoe of barbarians attempted to cordon off the baggage train and allow time for others to escape. Due to the cavalry and the desire for several legionaries to win riches, rather than just honour, from the engagement there were increasing breaks in the line. Unfortunately a host of warriors still stood between Maximus and his target. They raised their shields and spears upon seeing the centurion and his optio approach. Just as Maximus was about to issue the order for Apollo and his fellow few archers to start picking the enemy off, so he and Atticus could cut through the line, several Roman horsemen did the job for them. The warriors fortunate enough not to be cut down by razor sharp cavalry swords were skittled over by the horses.

"It is within the reach of every man to live nobly, but within no man's power to live long. Seneca. Or as another wise man once said, sometimes you've just got to get into the fight," Marcus Aurelius remarked with the hint of a smile, after turning his charger around to face the speechless centurion.

*

Due to the wealth of coin inside – and the fact that Balomar did not trust his warriors not to steal from him – the strongbox had been chained and padlocked to the wagon. Tarbus cursed his new ally, who had been keen to furnish him with orders rather than a key. The horses had long been commandeered so they could not ride the wagon back. Tarbus climbed on top of the vehicle though and brought down the heavy axe head upon a rusty section of the chain, roaring in frustration, hate and everything else as he did so.

Balloc and a dozen or so Arivisto warriors stood close by the wagon, acting as a last line of defence. They fidgeted with their weapons in their hands, either out of nervousness or from desire to use them. Their lips curled in up in disdain when they saw the two soldiers who had half burned down their village in front of them. A look of confidence and contempt was still visible behind the grime and dried blood on Rufus Atticus' face. Balloc, remembering his gesture after murdering Arrian, proceeded to raise his arms, open his mouth wide and waggle his tongue at the optio. Balloc briefly closed his eyes as he also let out a gargling battle cry, hoping to provoke the soldier into rushing into the fray. In a single fluid movement, however, Atticus drew one of his knives and threw it at the barbarian. The dagger smashed through his face, as if his open mouth had sucked in the polished blade. Balloc lifelessly fell to the ground, like a puppet whose strings had been cut.

"I never liked that bastard," Atticus drily remarked to his friend.

The Arivisto veterans had little time to be shocked, or to retaliate. Death whispered in their ears, as a flurry of arrows rained down on them from Apollo and his fellow archers. Some were killed immediately. Some retreated. A couple desperately jumped over the side of the bridge in an attempt to avoid the deadly missiles.

Maximus raised his hand to signal to cease firing.

Tarbus no longer had any thoughts for Balomar, the strongbox or even escaping. He just wanted to kill the Roman, cut down the man with his axe as if he were a tree that needed felling. His eyes bulged with rage, yet he walked towards the centurion as calmly as the centurion walked towards him.

"I am Tarbus of the Arivisto, a descendant of the Ariovistus, the *Scourge of Rome*," the barbarian proudly announced in Latin, thumping his chest, before swinging his giant battle-axe.

Tarbus cleverly lengthened the reach of his weapon by clasping the bottom of the shaft, but Maximus leaped out the way in time. The chieftain wore a well-crafted, reinforced breastplate over his fur jacket. His bare upper arms, which appeared flabby but were also packed with muscle, each possessed a tattoo of his beloved battle-axe.

The barbarian grinned wolfishly beneath his thick beard, believing that he had the measure and beating of the short sword carrying Roman. He swung his axe again and Maximus took cover behind the wagon. The centurion realised that it would be difficult for the point or edge of his gladius to penetrate his opponent's armour. So he altered his strategy.

When Tarbus swung his axe again Maximus quickly stepped inside, but rather than try to find a weak spot in his plate armour the centurion swiped his sword at the handle of the axe. Tarbus' low roar turned into a high pitched scream as the Roman cut off two fingers on his left hand. Blood pulsed out from the gruesome wound. Tarbus' eyes now bulged in shock, pain and grief as he gazed at the digits on the ground. It was now Maximus' turn to grin wolfishly. The weakened chieftain could no longer wield his heavy weapon effectively. When Tarbus next swung the weapon, with only one hand on the shaft, Maximus was able to easily avoid the blow – and then yank the axe away from his enemy. The soldier then slashed his sword across his opponent's left thigh, bringing the great chieftain to his knees.

"I'm Gaius Maximus, descendent of Lucius Oppius, the *Sword of Rome*. You murdered your son Junius Arrian – who was my friend," the praetorian coldly remarked, just before he stabbed his enemy through the neck.

Epilogue

Evening.

The breeze carried on it a strong scent of pine trees which could still, just, be recognised through the smell of smoke and the dead which stained the air. Maximus briefly looked to the clear, serene night sky - as a respite from the charnel house around him. Fires burned bodies. Wounded were being tended to. Wine soaked the throats for those who sung or talked of victory, or of fallen comrades.

The moon and stars seemed brighter to Maximus, as if they were new or closer. He recalled a phrase spoken by Julia the day before she passed away. "The light shines in the darkness, and the darkness comprehends it not." She said it was from one of the Gospels. Julia made Maximus promise that he would try and read the book after she had gone.

The centurion walked across the bridge with his Emperor. Both men felt mournful, yet also philosophical. The Danube shimmered in the moonlight.

"This is not the end Maximus. It is not even the beginning of the end. But it is, perhaps, the end of the beginning," Marcus Aurelius uttered, giving voice to his thoughts in regards to the long war ahead. "Already I have received messages from a number of Balomar's allies, or should I say former allies, requesting peace talks. We may all talk of peace but behind such words we will all still plan for war."

"You've defeated them once. You can do it again. Indeed after today the sight of your red cloak may be worth as much as half a cohort," the centurion drily remarked.

The Emperor permitted himself to smile, briefly.

"There will be talk of a triumph, no doubt. You may have to accompany me on the chariot Maximus, whisper that I am mortal. Others may prove too sycophantic and pour praise into my ear instead, except perhaps my wife. But this is just as much your triumph as mine. Indeed the victory belongs to all of us – and I will endeavour to use any spoils of war – or of peace treaties – to reward those who fought here today. I will also send what we can to the families of the wounded and dead. But, tell me, how can I reward you?"

"I'd ask that you grant a pension to Aurelia. She will need to be supported when she returns to Rome. I'd also like to request to escort her back to the capital myself."

Aurelius agreed to his requests and was cheered on the inside. When his friend spoke about the young woman there was a light in his eyes. He would tell Galen that perhaps Maximus now had something, or rather someone, to live for.

"I believe that Aurelia should be thankfully free from harm, in regards to those that wished to abduct her. I'm not so sure that you and I will be so fortunate as to escape future plots by our enemies, however," the Emperor said. "Can you also escort Galen back to Rome? He is presently attending to the wounded. But his place is in the capital. Not only do I feel more at ease, knowing that he can take care of Commodus should he fall ill – but he has his own great war to wage, against the plague. The victory of a cure will do more to save the Empire than a thousand battles in Pannonia."

*

At first he thought that it was the sound of a woodpecker but then Maximus realised the distant noise was that of legionaries hammering stakes into the ground to construct the fort. Aurelius had indeed crossed his Rubicon. The war would still be a long hard slog, but they were closer to victory now than they had been this morning. That was all one could ask for.

The centurion walked back to his tent, to find Atticus and young Apollo sharing a jug of wine. The legionary was listening to his optio talk about how he believed that the Empire was in decline. Apollo understood little – and maybe cared even less – but he nevertheless indulged his superior officer and pretended to be interested.

"...If the treasury keeps debasing the coinage then our currency will become worthless. And if the currency becomes worthless, everything will lose its value. Someone should tell the government that you cannot keep minting money as a cure-all to the problems of the economy... As both a state, and also as individuals, we have crippled ourselves with debt. We're like a man who, stuck in a hole, tries to dig deeper to get out. Sooner or later though the hole becomes his grave... Or our end will come Apollo from being taxed to death... For reasons of efficiency – and indeed freedom – you should be able to choose what you do with your money, rather than let a government, made up of over-bloated, self-serving bureaucrats, decide. Tax is as much the enemy as the Marcomanni. High taxes have been implemented not just to pay for the war, but rather to pay for a client state, populated by those who work for the government and those who receive their dole from it. Such are those numbers now that too many can and are persuaded into voting certain politicians into power – who further fuel high taxes, indebtedness and a client state... And then we have the problem of China. Gold is flowing out of the Empire as fast as the Danube to pay for Chinese silk, for dresses. But China seems content in hording its wealth, like Crassus, rather than using it to pay for Roman goods. Trade needs to be encouraged... And finally we have the war and the plague."

Atticus here paused to take a drink, and come up for air. Maximus had heard his friend's arguments many times before and felt that Apollo might need saving.

"Cease fire. I fear that you're depressing the lad. Or, worse, boring him. Don't worry, the Empire's not on its knees yet. You too should have some faith Atticus."

"Faith and wine are in short supply at the moment. The lights are going out all around the Empire," the optio replied. The usual glint in his eye had also dimmed, from talking about the possible decline and fall of Rome.

"It's never all doom and gloom though. The light shines in the darkness, and the darkness comprehends it not," Maximus said, quoting from a book that he had just started to read.

End Note

Sword of Empire: *Praetorian* is a work of fiction. There are both deliberate and unwitting historical inaccuracies throughout its pages. In particular, for dramatic reasons and due to scant resource material, I created my own narrative for the Battle of Pannonia. However, should you be interested in the history behind the fiction then I strongly recommend you read Frank McLynn's *Marcus Aurelius*: *Warrior*, *Philosopher*, *Emperor*. The book provides an engaging portrait of both the man and his times. Should you be tempted to read *The Meditations*, by Marcus Aurelius, then I recommend you give into temptation.

Please feel free to get in touch should you have enjoyed *Sword of Empire*: *Praetorian* – and thank you to readers who have been in contact in the past about my other books. I can be reached via richard@sharpebooks.com or through richardforemanauthor.com

Gaius Maximus and Rufus Atticus will return in *Sword of Empire*: *Centurion*.

Richard Foreman

*

Printed in Great Britain
by Amazon